The Mystery of The Barranca

Herman Whitaker

Alpha Editions

This edition published in 2024

ISBN : 9789361470059

Design and Setting By
Alpha Editions
www.alphaedis.com
Email - info@alphaedis.com

Contents

CHAPTER I

"

Oh Bob, just look at them!"

Leaning down from his perch on the sacked mining tools which formed the apex of their baggage, Billy Thornton punched his companion in the back to call his attention to a scene which had spread a blaze of humor over his own rich crop of freckles.

As a matter of fact, the spectacle of two men fondly embracing can always be depended on to stir the crude Anglo-Saxon sense of humor. In this case it was rendered still more ridiculous by age and portliness, but two years' wandering through interior Mexico had accustomed Thornton's comrade, Robert Seyd, to the sight. After a careless glance he resumed his contemplation of the crowd that thronged the little station. Exhibiting every variety of Mexican costume, from the plain white blanket of the peons to the leather suits of the rancheros and the hacendados, or owners of estates, it was as picturesque and brilliant in color and movement as anything in a musical extravaganza. The European clothing of a young girl who presently stepped out of the ticket office emphasized the theatrical flavor by its vivid contrast. She might easily have been the captive heroine among bandits, and the thought actually occurred to Billy. While she paused to call her dog, a huge Siberian wolf hound, she was hidden from Seyd's view by the stout embracers. Therefore it was to the dog that he applied Billy's remark at first.

"Isn't she a peach?"

She seemed the finest of her race that he had ever seen, and Seyd was just about to say that she carried herself like a "perfect lady" when the dissolution of the aforesaid embrace brought the girl into view. He stopped—with a small gasp that testified to his astonishment at her unusual type.

Although slender for her years—about two and twenty—her throat and bust were rounded in perfect development. The clear olive complexion was undoubtedly Spanish, yet her face lacked the firm line that hardens with the years. Perhaps some strain of Aztec blood—from which the Spanish-Mexican is never free—had helped to soften her features, but this would not account for their pleasing irregularity. A bit *rétroussée*, the small nose with its well-defined nostrils patterned after the Celtic. Had Seyd known it, the face in its entirety—colors and soft contours—is to be found to this day among the descendants of the sailors who escaped from the wreck of the Spanish Armada on the west coast of Ireland. Pretty and unusual as she was, her greatest charm centered in the large black eyes that shone amid her clear pallor, conveying in broad day the tantalizing mystery of a face seen for an instant through a warm gloaming. In the moment that he caught their velvet glance Seyd received an impression of vivacious intelligence altogether foreign in his experience of Mexican women.

As she was standing only a few feet away, he knew that she must have heard Billy's remark; but, counting on her probable ignorance of English, he did not hesitate to answer. "Pretty? Well, I should say—pretty enough to marry. The trouble is that in this country the ugliness of the grown woman seems to be in inverse ratio to her girlish beauty. Bet you the fattest hacendado is her father. And she'll give him pounds at half his age."

"Maybe," Billy answered. "Yet I'd be almost willing to take the chance."

As the girl had turned just then to look at the approaching train neither of them caught the sudden dark flash, supreme disdain, that drew an otherwise quite tender red mouth into a scarlet line. But for the dog they would never have been a whit the wiser. For as the engine came hissing along the platform the brute sprang and crouched on the tracks, furiously snarling, ready for a spring at the headlight, which it evidently took for the Adam's apple of the strange monster. The train still being under way, the poor beast's faith would have cost it its life but for Seyd's quickness. In the moment that the girl's cry rang out, and in less time than it took Billy to slide from his perch, Seyd leaped down, threw the dog aside, and saved himself by a spring to the cow-catcher.

"Oh, you fool! You crazy idiot!" While thumping him soundly, Billy ran on, "To risk your life for a dog—a Mexican's, at that!"

But he stopped dead, blushed till his freckles were extinguished, as the girl's voice broke in from behind.

"And the Mexican thanks you, sir. It was foolhardy, yes, and dearly as I love the dog I would not have had you take such a risk. But now that it is done—accept my thanks." As the stouter of the embracers now came bustling up, she added in Spanish, "My uncle, señor."

At close range she was even prettier; but, though gratitude had wiped out the flash of disdain, a vivid memory of his late remarks caused Seyd to turn with relief to the hacendado. During the delivery of effusive thanks he had time to cancel a first impression—gained from a rear view of a gaudy jacket—of a fat tenor in a Spanish opera, for the man's head and features were cast in a massive mold. His big fleshy nose jutted out from under heavy brows that overshadowed wide, sagacious eyes, Indian-brown in color. If the wind and weather of sixty years had tanned him dark as a peon, it went excellently with his grizzled mustache. Despite his stoutness and the costume, every fat inch of him expressed the soldier.

"My cousin, señor."

Having been placed, metaphorically, in possession of all the hacendado's earthly possessions, Seyd turned to exchange bows with a young man who had just emerged from the baggage-room—at least he seemed young at the first glance. A second look showed that the impression was largely due to a certain trimness of figure which was accentuated by the perfect fit of a suit of soft-dressed leather. When he raised his felt sombrero the hair showed thin on his temples. Neither were his poise and imperturbable manner attributes of youth.

"It was very clever of you, señor."

A slight peculiarity of intonation made Seyd look up. "Jealous," he thought, yet he was conscious of something else—some feeling too elusively subtle to be analyzed on the spur of the moment. Suggesting, as it did, that he had made a "gallery play," the remark roused in him quick irritation. But had it been possible to frame an answer there was no time, for just then the familiar cry, "*Vaminos!*" rang out, and the American conductor hustled uncle, niece, and her dog into the nearest car.

The entire incident had occupied little more than a moment, and as, a little bewildered by its rush, Seyd stood looking after the train he found himself automatically raising his cap in reply to a fluttering handkerchief.

"You Yankees are certainly very enterprising."

Turning quickly, Seyd met again the glance of subtle hostility. But, though he felt certain that the remark had been called forth by his salute, he had no option but to apply it to the mining kit toward which the other was pointing.

"You are for the mines, señor? In return for your service to my cousin it is, perhaps, that I can be of assistance—in the hiring of men and mules?"

While equally quiet and subtle, the patronage in his manner was easier to meet. Undisturbed, however, when Seyd declined his offer, he sauntered quietly away.

"*Bueno!* As you wish."

CHAPTER II

"

I'll be with you in a minute, folks."

To appreciate the accent which the American station agent laid on "folks" it is necessary that one should have been marooned for a couple of years in a ramshackle Mexican station with only a chocolate-skinned henchman, or *mozo*, for companion. It asserted at once welcome and patriotic feeling.

"You know this isn't the old United States," he added, hurrying by. "These greasers are the limit. Close one eye for half a minute and when you open it again it's a cinch you'll find the other gone. If they'd just swipe each other's baggage it wouldn't be so bad. But they steal their own, then sue the company for the loss. Here, you sons of burros, drop that!" with which he dived headlong into the midst of the free fight that a crowd of *cargadores*, or porters, were waging over the up train baggage.

Taking warning, the two returned to their own baggage. As they waited, talking, these two closest of friends offered a fairly startling contrast. In the case of Seyd, a graduate in mining of California University, years of study and strain had tooled his face till his aggressive nose stood boldly out above hollowed cheeks and black-gray eyes. A trifle over medium height, the hundred and sixty pounds he ought to have carried had been reduced a good ten pounds by years of prospecting in Mexico and Arizona. This loss of flesh, however, had been more than made up by a corresponding gain in muscle. Moving a few paces around the baggage, he exhibited the easy, steady movement that comes from the perfect co-ordination of nerve and muscle. His feet seemed first to feel, then to take hold of the ground. In fact, his entire appearance conveyed the impression of force under perfect control, ready to be turned loose in any direction.

Shorter than Seyd by nearly half a foot, Billy Thornton, on the other hand, was red where the other was dark, loquacious instead of thoughtful. From his fiery shock of red hair and undergrowths of red stubble to his slangy college utterance he proved the theory of the attraction of opposites. Bosom friends at college, it had always been understood between them that when either got his "hunch" the other should be called in to share it. And as the luck—in the shape of a rich copper mine—had come first to Seyd, he had immediately wired for Billy. They were talking it over, as they so often before had done, when the agent returned.

"Why—you're the fellow that was down here last fall, ain't you?" he asked, offering his hand. "Didn't recognize you at first. You don't mean to say that you have denounced—"

"—The Santa Gertrudis prospect?" Seyd nodded. "He means the opposition I told you we might expect." He answered Billy's look of inquiry.

"Opposition!" The agent spluttered. "That's one word for it. But since you're so consarnedly cool about it, mister, let me tell you that this makes the eleventh time that mine has been denounced, and so far nobody has succeeded in holding it." Looking at Billy, probably as being the more impressionable, he ran on: "The first five were Mex and as there were no pesky foreign consuls to complicate the case with bothersome inquiries, they simply vanished. One by one they came, hit the trail out there in a cloud of dust, and were never seen again.

"After them came the Dutchman, a big fat fellow, obstinate as one of his own mules, and a scrapper. For a while it looked as though he'd make good—might have, perhaps, if he hadn't taken to using his dynamite box for a pillow. You see, his peons used to steal the sticks to fish, and so many of them blew themselves into kingdom come that he was always running shy on labor. So, as I say, he used the box for a pillow till it went off one night and distributed him all over the Barranca de Guerrero. Just how it came about of course nobody knew, nor cared, and they never did find a piece big enough to warrant an inquest. It just went as accidental, and he'd scarcely, so to say, stopped raining before a Frenchman jumped the claim. But he only lasted for a couple of days, landed back here within a week, and jumped the up train without a word.

"Last came the English Johnnies, two of 'em, the real 'haw, haw' boys; no end of style to them and their outfit. As they had hosts of friends up Mexico City, it would never have done to use harsh measures. But if the Johnnies had influence of one sort, Don Luis—he's the landowner, you know—had it to burn of another. Not only did he gain a general's commission during the revolutionary wars, but he's also a member of the Mexican Congress, so close to the government that he needs only to wink to get what he wants. So just about the time the Johnnies had finished development work and begun to deliver ore out here at the railroad—presto! freights went up, prices went down, till they'd wiped out the last cent of profit. Out go the Johnnies—enter you." With real earnestness he concluded: "Of course, there's nothing I'd like better than to have you for neighbors. It ain't so damn lively here. But I'd hate to see you killed. Take my advice, and quit."

He had addressed himself principally to Billy. But instead of discouragement, impish delight illumined the latter's freckles.

"A full-sized general with the whole Mexican government behind him? Bully! I never expected anything half so good. But, say! If the mine is so rich why don't the old cock work it himself instead of leaving it to be denounced by any old tramp?"

"Because he don't have to. He has more money now than he ever can use. He is worth half a million in cattle alone. And he's your old-fashioned sort that hate the very thought of change. By the way, he just left on the up train, him and his niece."

"What, the girl with the dog?" Billy yelled it. "Didn't you see—no, you were in the baggage-room. Well, he's our dearest friend—presented Seyd here with all of his horses, cattle, lands, and friends. A bit of a mining claim ought not to cut much ice in an order like that."

"You met them?" The agent shook his head, however, after he had heard the particulars. "Don't count much on Spanish courtesies. They go no deeper than the skin. Nice girl, the niece, more like us than Mex, and she ain't full-blood, for matter of that. Her grandfather was Irish, a free lance that fought with Diaz during the French war. His son by a Mexican wife married Don Luis's sister, and when he died she and her daughter came to keep the old fellow's house, for he's been a widower these twenty years. Like most of the sprigs of the best Mexican families, she was educated in Europe, so she speaks three languages—English, French, and Spanish. Yes, they're nice people from the old Don down, but lordy! how he hates us gringos. He'll repay you for the life of the dog—perhaps by saving you alive for a month? But after that—take my advice, and git."

While he was talking, Seyd had listened with quiet interest. Now he put in, "We will—just as quickly as we can hire men and burros to pack our stuff out to the mine."

"Well, if you will—you will." Having thus divested himself of responsibility, the agent continued: "And here's where your troubles begin. Though donkey-drivers are as thick as fleas in this town, I doubt whether you can hire one to go to Santa Gertrudis."

"But the Englishmen?" Seyd questioned. "They must have had help."

"Brought their entire outfit down with them from Mexico City."

After Seyd's rejection of his offer the hacendado had entered into conversation with a ranchero at the other end of the platform, and, glancing a little regretfully in his direction, Seyd asked, "Do you know him?"

The agent nodded. "Sebastien Rocha? Yes, he's a nephew to the General."

"He offered to get me mules."

"He did! Why, man alive! he hates gringos worse than—worse than I hate Mexicans. *He* offered you help? I doubt he'll do it when he knows where you're going." In a last attempt at dissuasion he added, "But if he doesn't I can't see how you can win out with rates and prices at the same mark that wiped out the Johnnies."

"That's our business." Seyd laughed. Then, warmed by the honest fellow's undoubted anxiety, he said, "Do you remember any consignment of brick that ever came to this station?"

"Sure, three car loads, billed to the Dutchman. But what has that to do—"

"Just this—that the man had the right idea. Though the mine is the richest copper proposition I have ever seen—besides carrying gold values sufficient to cover smelting expenses—it would never pay, as you say, to ship it out at present prices. But once smelted down into copper matte there's a fortune in it, as the Dutchman knew. He had already laid out the foundation of an old-style Welsh smelter, and, though it isn't very big, we propose to make it stake us to a modern plant."

"So that's your game!" The agent whistled.

"That's our game," Billy confirmed. "If dear cousin over there can only be persuaded to furnish the mules we will do the rest. Go ask him, Bob."

Seyd hesitated. "I'm afraid that I turned him down rather roughly. Let's try first ourselves."

For the last half hour their baggage had formed a center of interest for the porters, mule-drivers, and hackmen who formed the bulk of the crowd, and the snap of the agent's fingers brought a score of them running. Each tried to make his calling and election sure by seizing a piece of baggage. In ten seconds the pile was dissolved and was flowing off in as many different directions when Seyd's answer to a question brought all to a sudden halt.

"To the *mina* Santa Gertrudis."

Crash! the kit of mining tools dropped from the shoulder of the muleteer who had asked the question, and it had no more than touched earth before it was buried under the other pieces.

"I told you so," the agent commented, and was going on when a voice spoke in from their rear.

"What is the trouble, señors?"

The hacendado had approached unnoticed, and, turning quickly, Seyd met for the third time the equivocal look, now lightened by a touch of amusement. Suppressing a recurrence of irritation he answered, quietly: "We wish to go to the hacienda San Nicolas, señor, upon which we have denounced the mining claim known as the Santa Gertrudis. For some reason no one of these men will hire. Perhaps you can tell why?"

"Now your fat's in the fire," the agent muttered.

Whether or no he had overheard Seyd's answer to the muleteer, the man's dark face gave no sign. "*Quien sabe?* Ask their blood brother, the burro. One would have little to do and time to waste if he attempted to plumb a mule-driver's superstitions. *Ola*, Carlos."

While he was talking the crowd had continued to back away, but it stopped now and stood staring, for all the world like a herd of frightened cattle. The big muleteer who had led the retreat returned on a shuffling run, and as he stood before the hacendado, sombrero in hand, Seyd saw the fear in his face.

"This fellow sometimes works for me. You will need"—he paused, overlooking the baggage—"three burros and two riding-mules. He has only two. *Ola*, Mattias!" When a second muleteer had come with the same breathless haste he gave the quiet order, "You will take these señors to Santa Gertrudis."

Bowing slightly, he had walked away before Seyd could lay hands on enough Spanish to state his obligation, and as, pausing, he then looked back his face once more changed, expressing knowledge and sarcastic amusement at the mixed feelings behind Seyd's halting thanks. His bow, returning the customary answer, was more than half shrug.

"It is nothing."

"One moment, señor!"

The burrors having departed with their loads, Seyd and Billy were mounting to follow when the hacendado called to them from the platform. "To-night, of course, you will stay in Chilpancin. But to-morrow? By which trail do you travel?" When Seyd answered he added a word of counsel: "I thought so. Most strangers take that way. But there is a shorter by many miles. Instruct your drivers to take the old trail down the Barranca."

Thanking him, they rode on.

In accordance with the mysterious and immutable law which places all Mexican cities at least a mile from the railroad, they traveled nearly half an hour before sighting, across a barranca, the town cuddled in a hollow beneath the opposite hills. Under the rich light of the waning sun the variegated color of its walls, houses, churches, merged in warm gold, glowed like a topaz in the setting of the dark hills. Paved with river cobbles and crooked as a dog's hind leg, a street fell steeply down into the barranca from whose black depths uprose the low roar of rushing waters. Entering upon it, while still within sound of a freight engine puffing upgrade to the station, they dropped back four hundred years into the midst of a life that differed but little from that of the Aztecs under the Montezumas.

On both sides of the street one-story adobes flamed in all the colors of the rainbow—roses, purples, umber, greens—a vivid alternation which was toned only by the weathered gray of heavy doors and massive oaken grills across the windows. At the tinkle of their bells there would come a flash of Spanish eyes in the cool dusk behind the windows, and a pretty face would emerge from deep shadow to fade again before Billy's smile. The peons and hooded women on the narrow causeways were equally reserved. They either passed without according them notice or returned to their glances a stolid stare. Theirs were the dark, impenetrable faces of old Mexico.

While they were climbing at a snail's pace the opposite hill, dusk fell over the town, but presently, riding out of a black alley into the main plaza, they emerged on a scene that caused even the matter-of-fact Billy to exclaim in wonder. On all four sides hundreds of torches blossomed in the dusk, toning with soft rich lights the vivid adobes, tinting the cold white blankets and garments of the hucksters who squatted by their displays—guavas and pineapples, cocoanuts, mangoes, alligator pears, and other fruits of the tropics which shared the same straw mat with cabbage, squash, onions, and other familiar produce of the cold North. In accordance with the shrewd policy that has always kept the Roman Church in close touch with its world, the booths extended to the very doors of a stone church which occupied one side of the square, and the heavy odors of fried garlic mingled with the breath of incense that floated out through the wide doors.

A religious fiesta was in full blast, and they had to turn the mules to avoid the stream of worshipers who shuffled across the square, up the stone steps, and the length of the paved aisles to the great altar which blazed with the light of a thousand candles. Looking, as they rode past, they saw a peon—whose spotless blanket shone whiter by contrast with the scarlet serape which had fallen backward across his calves—erect on his knees, arms extended in a rigid cross, a figure of deathless adoration before the Virgin. It required only the brazen storm of bells that just then broke overhead to complete the atmosphere of savage medievalism. The worshipers might easily have been the first Aztec converts crawling before the superior altars of the Spanish conquerors' God.

Seyd, always thoughtful and sensitive to impression, felt the influence of the scene, and the feeling deepened as their mules struck hollow echoes in the vaulted passage of the hotel whose iron-studded gates, barred windows, yard-thick walls all bespoke a life which had not yet progressed beyond the era of sieges. A runway led down into a wide courtyard and to the stables which lay under a tiled gallery, the hotel proper, for the cell-like sleeping-rooms used by the better class opened upon it.

But the real life of the place surged in the patio, or courtyard, below, and, after they had dined on rice, eggs, and beans, or frijoles, Billy and Seyd perched on the balustrade of the gallery to watch its ebb and flow. Into the great stone inclosure muleteers of Tepic, freighters of Guadalajara, potters of Cuernavaca and Taxco, pilgrims to the far shrines, and their first cousins in dirt and importunity, the beggars, had poured from three main lines of travel, and they were so crowded that it was difficult to find space among the mule panniers, crates, and bundles for their tiny cooking-fires. On occasion a face, plump and darkly pretty, would bloom out of the dusk as a woman fanned the charcoal under her clay cooking-pots. Again, a leaping flame would illumine a hawk face, deeply bronzed and heavily mustached, or lend a deeper dye to the scarlet of some sleeper's serape. In its rich somber color the scene made a picture that would have been loved by Rembrandt. Just as it had done for centuries before the great master was born to his brush, the scene changed and mingled, ebbed and flowed, while its units passed among the fires, exchanging the gossip of the trails. The hum of it rose to the gallery like the low roar of a distant torrent, but out of it Seyd was able to catch and translate isolated scraps.

"Take not thy *aguardiente* to El Quiss, *amigo*. The administrador—I tell it to my ruth, since I was well skinned by him—is a thief of the nether world. He would flay a flea for the hide and fat."

"*Ola*, Carlos! The *jefe* [chief of police] of San Pedro is keeping an eye for thy return ever since he bought the last load of charcoal."

"The swine! Is it my fault that he expects good oak burning for the price of soft ceiba?"

One remark caused Seyd to prick his ears, for it was addressed to one of their own muleteers. "Where go the gringos, *amigo*? To Santa Gertrudis? And thou art driving for them? *Hombre*, hast thou so little regard for thy neck?"

The answer was lost in the sudden braying of a burro in the stables underneath, but the voice of the questioner, a strident tenor, rose over all. "An order from Don Sebastien? *Carambar-r-r-a!* And you go by the old trail down the Barranca? But, *hombre!* It is—" The voice lowered so that Seyd could not hear.

Imagining that the talk bore merely on the condition of the trail, he dismissed it from his mind and returned to his study of the crowd, permitting his gaze to wander here, there, wherever the incessant movement brought to the surface some bit of color or trait of life. In this he obeyed a natural instinct. Endowed with a temperament nicely balanced between the philosophical and the practical, he had taken an auxiliary course in "letters" along with his mining for the sole purpose of broadening his viewpoint and widening his touch with life. Indeed, he had bent his profession to the same end, using it as a means to travel and study, in which he differed altogether from Billy, who was the mining engineer in every dimension. Where Billy saw only the externals, humors, and absurdities, and the picturesqueness of that teeming life, Seyd's subtle intelligence took hold of the primordial feeling under it all. Contributing only an occasional answer to the other's chatter, he bathed in the atmosphere and absorbed the wild medievalism of it while reviewing in thought the events of the day. The girl and her dog, her uncle the General, Don Sebastien the hacendado—the latter was in his mind when the sudden leaping of a fire at the far end of the patio revealed his face.

"Look!" But in the moment Seyd grasped Billy's arm the blaze fell. "I thought I saw him—that fellow, Sebastien—talking to Carlos, our mule-driver."

"Well, why not?" Billy answered. "I gathered that he lives far out. Like ourselves, probably too far to start out to-night."

"Of course." Seyd nodded. "He just happened to be in my mind. Only why should he be in talk with our mule-driver?"

"Search me." Billy shrugged. "But if he was, it is easy to prove it. There's Carlos now. Call him up here."

The muleteer, when questioned a minute later, shook his head. "No, señor, Don Sebastien is not here. He rode out at sunset, is now leagues away on the trail."

If he were lying, his brown stolid face gave no sign; and, having given him his orders for next day, Seyd returned to his study of the crowd. He had forgotten the incident by the time Billy dragged him away to bed.

CHAPTER III

"

If we are on the road at daybreak we shall reach the Barranca early in the afternoon," Seyd had said, commenting on his order to the mule-driver. But, fagged out by the day's hot travel, they did not awaken until a slender beam of light stole between the iron window bars and laid a golden finger across Billy's eyes.

"We shall have to hustle now." Seyd concluded a diatribe on the Mexican *mozo* in general while they were dressing. "For you must see the Barranca by daylight. Without its naked savagery it is as big and grand as the Colorado Cañon. Besides, if this trail is as dizzy a proposition as the one I went by on the last trip, I'd rather not tackle it after dark."

It would have been just as well, however, had they taken their time, for after breakfast came Carlos with a tale of cast-off shoes. It was Paz and Luz, the mules the señors were riding! And having roundly cursed the memory of the fool wife who had been induced by an apparently innocent colthood to bestow names of beauty like Peace and Light upon such misbegotten devils, Carlos further informed them:

"Never were there such ungrateful brutes, señors. Not content with the good barley I had just fed him, Paz it is that takes a piece out of Padre Celso's arm one fine day and so gets me cursed with candle and Book. And the curse sticks, señors, working itself out by means of this devil of a light who, within one week, chooses the fat belly of the *jefe* of Tehultepec as a cushion for his heels. A year's earnings that trick cost me, not to mention the prettiest set of blue stripes that ever warmed a cold back. Neither is there a tree between San Blas and the Arroyo Grande that they have not used to scrape off a load. But this shall be the end. They shall feel the knife in their throats at the end of this trip." In the mean time would the señors be pleased to wait for an hour?

There being no other choice, the señors would, and, returning to their last night's perch on the balustrade, they watched the patio disgorge its dark life upon the street. Shining in over the low-tiled roofs, the sunlight struck and was thrown back by the massive golden walls on the opposite side in a flood that set fire to brilliant serapes, illumined silver buttons, filled the whole place with light and cheer. Not to mention their interest in the saddling and packing of the loads—to which some refractory mule contributed an occasional humorous touch—a comedy was invariably enacted between the fat landlord and the departing travelers, for only after an altercation which always required the witness of all the saints to the reasonableness of his charges were the gates swung open. With much haggling and confusion of crackling oaths they went out, one by one, *cargadores* and peons, beggars and pilgrims, the tinkling mule trains with their quaint freights, and not until the last hoof struck on the cobbles did Seyd think to look at his watch.

"Nine o'clock. What has become of those—"

Fortunately they arrived at that moment with Paz and Luz, the damned and foredoomed, and a quarter of an hour thereafter their bells tinkled pleasantly in the scrub oak and copal which first climbed with the trail up a ravine behind the town and then led on through fields where corn grew, by some green miracle thrusting stout green stalks between the stones.

Though it was still quite early in the day, heat waves trembled all over the land. The somnolent hum of insect life, the whisper of a light wind in the corn, were alike conducive to sleep. Before they had been riding an hour both began to yawn. The sibilant hiss of the muleteers urging the mules grew fainter in Seyd's ears, and, though he was conscious in a dim way that the trail had led out from the fields and was falling, falling, falling downhill through growths of cactus and mimosa into the copal woods, he drowsed on till an exclamation from Billy aroused him to a grisly sight—the dozen and odd mummies whose withered limbs clicked in the breeze as they swung by the neck from the wide boughs of a banyan.

"*Bandidos*, señor, thieves and cutthroats." The bigger of the two muleteers answered Seyd's question. "They were hanged by Don Sebastien."

"Why, that's our friend back at the station." Billy commented on Seyd's translation. "I'm sure that was the name the agent gave him."

"*Si*, señor," the mule-driver confirmed the impression. "And these are but the tithe of those that he hanged. For years the whole of this country was overrun with *bandidos* who took advantage of the absence of the principal men at the wars to rob and murder at will. They were levying regular tolls on the rancheros and hacendados when Don Sebastien returned from his schooling. Though only a lad of two and twenty, he began by hanging the bandits' messenger in the gates of his hacienda, an act that all thought would end by the wiping of the very memory of the place from the face of the earth. But instead of waiting to be attacked Don Sebastien took the stoutest of his peons and went out after the thieves. And he kept after them all that winter, the following summer, into the next year. No trail was too long, wet, or weary if he could mark its end with a brigand swinging under a tree. Here, there, everywhere within a hundred miles of his hacienda of El Quiss he hanged them by twos and threes and left them to swing in the wind, and it speaks for the fear in which he came to be held that no man, father, mother, sister, or lover dared to cut one down. Scarce a cross trail in this country that lacks its warning, and through his rigor it came to pass that you, señors, might now leave your purses on the open highway where a dozen years ago you would surely have left your lives. No man would dare touch—"

"—Except Don Sebastien," Seyd put in, laughing.

But the man returned only a stare. "What use would he have of purses, señor, that has so many of his own?"

"Perhaps to give to the Church." But he stopped laughing, surprised by the sudden cloud that spread on the man's face.

"Never! Though he has a church on his own hacienda, Don Sebastien never crosses its threshold. And Mattias, here, can tell you of the talk he gives to the priest."

"*Si! si!*" In his eagerness to share the limelight the fellow almost shook off his head. "It is, see you, that I am delivering a mule load of charcoal at El Quiss on the very day that Don Sebastien hires the priest. You are to see him, as I did, sitting on the gallery above the courtyard puffing his cigar in such wise—was there ever such irreverence!—that the smoke rises in the face of the padre who stands before him. And his voice comes ringing down to where Miguel, the steward, is trying to beat me down a peso on the price of the charcoal. 'I have built you a church, and for performing the offices I shall pay you one hundred silver pesos the month, for, though I did not feel, myself, any need of your mutterings, they serve to keep my people quiet. Over them you shall exercise the usual authorities, and you may come and go at will through the hacienda—all but one place. If after this hour I find that your foot has touched my threshold I'll hang you in its gates.' Thus he spoke, señor, and he would have done it—to a priest quicker than a bandit, for of the two it is hard to tell that which he hates the most."

"Hum!" Billy coughed when Seyd had translated. Jerking his thumb at the grisly witnesses to the tale's truth, he commented: "I now begin to understand the general respect for our friend. A man who does things like that is entitled to some consideration. Let us be thankful for pump guns and automatics. If this had been the day of the old muzzle-loader I'm darned if I'd have tackled your hunch."

In the next hour the red-tiled colored adobe hamlets of the small farmers began to give place to the *jacals* of the country, flimsy huts with sides of cane stalks and grass-thatched. Then the trail passed out from the eternal succession of corn and *maguey* fields into wastes of volcanic scoria, where it began presently to climb mountains, for no apparent reason except to fall dizzily into shallow valleys which were sparsely timbered with copal and other soft woods. In one valley they came upon an Aztec ruin. A huge parallelogram in shape, it was more than half buried and so overgrown with brush and creepers that they would have passed without notice if the trail had not happened to run along the face of one wall. Looking closely, Seyd first observed a monstrous squat figure in bas-relief, one of dozens which were interwoven into an intricate design; then, riding along, he saw frightfully distorted faces peering out from behind a green veil of creepers. Broad and fat, long and thin, some were stretched in a wide grin, others thrust out tongues in ribald mockery. Here the eyes of one were distorted in a painful squint. There a slant upturn of tight-drawn lids revealed the quintessence of priestly cruelty. Another was grossly lewd. Through anger, violence, lust, fear, the expressions ran the gamut of passion to its death in the cold face of the god whose enormous image formed the corner. The oblong ears, triangular eyes and nose, parallel lips, were such as a child loves to draw on a slate, yet on that enormous scale their mathematical lines somehow conveyed an impression of absolute force. The Sphynx-like calm of the face stirred Seyd's imagination with pictures of captives led to the Aztec altars. Even practical Billy was moved to remark:

"Those old chaps couldn't have been very nice neighbors."

"No; and they are the lineal ancestors of the neighbors we shall have presently." Later the thought was to recur under conditions that would lend it enormous force. He forgot it in the moment of utterance, saying, as he glanced at his watch: "We have been doing pretty well. At this rate we'll make the Barranca quite early."

He had failed to allow, however, for the demon which, usually content with the complete possession of Paz and Luz, suddenly entered into the burros and sent them flying downhill through a grove of trees. Entering on one side fully loaded, they emerged at the other naked, and by the time they were rounded up and reloaded Seyd had to recast his schedule.

"We'll be lucky if we make it now in daylight. We may have to camp at the top."

Repeated in Spanish, the latter suggestion drew vigorous headshakes from both muleteers. Carlos made answer. "No, señor, at this time of the year one would perish of the cold, and there is an inn in the Barranca with the finest of accommodations. The trail? It is nothing! A peso for every time I have traveled it by night would buy me a rancho—and Paz and Luz, devils as they are, could travel it blindfold." And whether, as Billy suggested, they were afraid of missing their usual communion with the fleas in the inn stables, both he and Mattias began to hustle the mules with oaths, hissings, whip-crackings. They kept after them so hard that the train trotted out of a forest of upland piñon upon the rim of a great valley a full half hour before sundown.

Though prepared by Seyd's descriptions for something unusually fine, Billy's blue eyes opened to the limit, and he sat silent upon his mule, staring, altogether bereft of his usual loquacity. From their feet the land broke suddenly and fell into purple depths from which dark hills uplifted ruddy peaks into the blaze of the setting sun. The Barranca was so deep, so vast in scale, that he grew dizzy in following with his eye the tiny zigzag of the trail down, down, till it was lost in blue haze through which even the giant ceibas and tall cedars showed like microscopic plants. Across the valley, miles away, naked mountains tossed and tumbled, seamed, scarred, gashed by slide and quake, sterile and desolate, as on the far day that some world convulsion raised them out of the sea.

"Drunk! drunk!" Billy breathed, at last. "Nature gone on a jag. Drunken mountains loose in a crazy world. The whole earth is turned on edge. Hold me, Bob, before I fall in. How deep do you call this bit of a hole?"

"About five thousand feet down to the floor. It falls off a thousand and more in a few miles to the coast. You see, we are still in touch with the old Pacific. Can't be more than thirty miles or so down to the sea."

"The dear old pond. Isn't that pine on the other side?"

"Sure. An American company is taking out millions of feet, a hundred or so miles farther up. That's a great old tree, and quite particular about the company it keeps. Look how sharply it draws the line along the slope, lifting its skirts from the contamination of the tropics. That spark of green in the far distance is sugar cane—two thousand acres of it on the General's hacienda of San Nicolas. And you see the gash over there, all yellow and green, about three thousand feet down from the top—that is us, señor, the *mina* Santa Gertrudis. And that reminds me—we'll have to be moving if we are to make the inn before midnight. *Vaminos*, Carlos."

But the muleteer shook his head. "After you, señor, for if these devils should take to running again, not in six months should we fish your baggage out of the cañons."

Leading down the trail, which zigzagged along the faces of a V-shaped wall, Seyd perceived, as he thought, the soundness of the argument, for at the first turn a stone from his mule's foot dropped five hundred feet plumb before rebounding into greater depths, and at no place did the width of the path allow an unnecessary inch for the swing of the packs. Deceived by the succession of stairways through which the trail dropped down to the thin thread that marked its course along the bottoms, Billy objected:

"Three hours, you say? Looks to me as though we could make it in one."

"Less than that—if your mule should happen to slip and take it sideways. Let me see—allowing a thousand feet to a bump, about fourteen seconds ought to distribute you nicely among the bottom trees. But if you elect to follow me around the eight or nine miles of trail you cannot see, it will take the full three hours."

Even while he was speaking the ruddy fires on the valley hills were suddenly extinguished, only the stark peaks on the other side lifted like yellow torches in the last blaze. One by one these also went out, and another hour found them journeying in gloom that was intensified rather than lightened by the section of moon which achieved a precarious balance on the rim above. In darkness and silence that was broken only by the scrape of hoofs and rattle of displaced stones they followed down and down and down, until Billy presently came under a singular hallucination. Repeatedly he put out his hand to repel the rock wall that seemed to be animated with a desire to crowd him off into the cañon, and because of this pardonable nervousness he endured a real trial that would have drawn a quick protest from Seyd—to wit, the senseless way in which the muleteers were driving their beasts on his heels. Twice he rapped a rough nose that tried to force its way in between him and the wall, and he breathed more easily when an easier grade permitted them to draw ahead on a gentle trot.

Accustomed, on his part, to leave all to his beast, Seyd rode with a loose bridle, lost in thought, his mind busy with mining plans. And thus it was that when Paz suddenly stopped, snorting, at the end of a trot which had carried them well ahead of the train around a rock wall, he almost went over her head. Recovering quickly, he was about to drive in the spurs; and a man of slower intuitions would surely have done it. With him, however, action invariably preceded thought, from instincts almost as acute as those which had brought the mule to a stop. Dismounting, he stepped ahead. Then, to the horror of Billy, who heard the burros slipping and sliding as they came round the wall on a trot, his voice came back.

"Hold on, there! A slide has carried away the trail!"

CHAPTER IV

Although he had always doubted the phenomenon, Billy's hair stood on end, and when, in the face of Seyd's shouts in Spanish to stop, the burros still came on he felt his cap move.

"Billy!" Seyd's command rang out sharply. "Dismount and lie down. It's our only chance."

In that tense moment, however, Mr. William Thornton, assayer and metallurgist, had done an amount of thinking that would have required many minutes of his leisure. He was already on the ground, and as he lay there, arms wrapped over the back of his head as a protection against the sharp hoofs that would presently grind his face in the dust, uncomfortable expectation gave birth to inspiration. As Seyd also braced himself for the shock there came the scratch of a match, and Billy's red head flashed out in relief against the belly of the leading burro as it upreared in fright at the blaze. In the same moment a second blunt head shoved itself like a wedge between the first burro and the wall, and as the gray body shot off sideways into the chasm Seyd saw first the others sliding in a desperate effort to stop, and behind them the mule whips swinging to drive them on. As under a flashlight it all flamed out and vanished.

In the short time required for Billy to strike a second match Seyd's mind registered an astonishing number of impressions. A hoarse yell, a sudden scurry of departing hoofs, and Billy's hysterical profanity formed merely the background of a sequence that flashed back over the events of the day. The scraps of muleteers' talk the night before, the runaway, and other minor delays, the drivers' refusal to camp on the rim, their insistence that he and Billy should take the lead, all fused in a belief which he expressed as the second match flaring up showed the trail empty of life between themselves and the next turn.

"It's a frame-up! They knew of the slide. They had it fixed to run us off in the dark."

"But where are they now?" Billy gazed down into the dark void. "Surely they didn't all go over."

"No such luck. The burros bolted back on them, and they just legged it out of the way. Listen!" A scurry of hoofs sounded on the level above. "There they go, and it's up to us to keep them going. Back your mule up and turn. If we don't give them the run of their lives we'll deserve all they tried to give us."

And run they did. Overtaking the burros just as they began to slow down, Seyd slipped ahead, struck a match close to the tail of the last, and so precipitated the cavalcade once more upon the sweating drivers. Whereafter, they took turns and kept the frightened beasts on a breathless trot up the heartbreaking grades. Under the flare of a match they sometimes caught a glimpse of the muleteers shuffling ahead on a tired run. Occasionally their sobbing breath rose over the scrape of the hoofs. But first one riding, then the other, they hustled them on without mercy till the train opened at last upon the plateau above.

"Now, then! Run them down!" Seyd shouted; but as he swung his mule out to go by the burros he almost ran into a horseman who had just reined his beast to one side of the trail.

"It is you, señor?"

Here on the top the light of the stars helped out the weak moon, and, though the man's face was in shadow, Seyd recognized the upright, graceful figure. "Come to see if the job is done." He thought it while answering aloud, "As you perceive, señor."

"Not until long after you left did I hear of the break in the trail, and I have ridden hard—used up one horse and half killed this poor beast. But no matter so long as I am in time."

"Hypocrite!" Seyd thought again. A little nonplussed, however, by the tone of assurance, he gave his thought lighter expression. "You would not have been if these fellows had had their way."

"*Caramba*, señor! Why?"

If his surprise were assumed it was certainly remarkably well done. While Seyd was telling of their narrow escape he sat his horse, silent but attentive. With the last word he burst into a fury of action. Uttering a Spanish oath, he drove in the spurs and rode his rearing horse straight at the mule-drivers, who had turned on Billy with drawn knives, lashing them with his heavy quirt over face, head, shoulders. Five minutes later his whip was still cutting the air with a shrill whistle, and, richly as the fellows deserved it, Seyd and Billy shuddered at the pitiless flogging. Strangest to them of all, the men endured this without attempt at flight or resistance. They stood, their arms shielding their faces, whimpering like beaten hounds.

It was their abject submissiveness that injected a touch of doubt into Billy's comment. "It looks, after all, as though they had done it themselves."

Seyd shrugged. "Perhaps; in any case we have no proof."

"Now, blind swine, that will serve for a while!" Sebastien's cold voice broke in. "Off with you and build a fire, then stake out the mules." Seyd's suspicion gave a little more before his quiet assurance. "You will have to stay here till morning, señors, for it is many miles along the rim to the other trail. Unfortunately, it was your supply mule that went into the cañon, so you must needs go hungry. However, we have a proverb, 'A warm fire helps the empty belly,' and to-morrow you will be able to recover your goods."

Neither did his expression, as presently revealed by the fire, offer evidence for doubt. As he stood looking down at the blaze Seyd was vividly reminded of the Aztec god, for its cold stone face was not more inscrutable than this quiet brown mask. Its inscrutability provoked him to ask a sudden question.

"Did I not see you at the hotel last night?"

But the sudden challenge produced only an indifferent shrug. "Perhaps. I was there."

He did look up at Billy's vigorous comment on his answer as translated by Seyd: "Then why didn't he show himself this morning? Goodness knows we left late enough."

He even asked, "What does he say?" And the sense having been softened in translation to an expression of mild wonder at his non-appearance, he quietly replied, "I do not doubt that the señor's departure was fraught with enormous significance for the country at large, but not being informed of it, there was no reason for me to cut my sleep."

Though the smile which marked his appreciation of the blush that drowned out Billy's freckles when Seyd translated was so slight as to be almost imperceptible, it yet increased his anger. "The dago!" he growled. "I'd punch his head for five cents Mex. The gall of him! Standing there poking fun at us after we have just missed death at the hands of his brigands. And you really think that he planned it all?"

"Looks like it. He chose the men, the trail. Was seen last night at the hotel. Appears now at the psychological moment. Any jury would—"

"—Pronounce me guilty. They would be mistaken, sir."

Utterly confounded at the interruption which was delivered in fluent English—so surprised, indeed, that Billy glanced around to make sure that nobody else had spoken—they stared at him across the fire in red confusion. When Seyd at last found his tongue he could only stammer the obvious question, "You speak English?"

"As you perceive, sir." As he returned Seyd his phrase of a few minutes before not even a twinkle betrayed his knowledge of their ridiculous situation.

Nor was one needed to increase Billy's anger. "Then why don't you speak it?" he roughly blurted.

Ignoring the question, the man went on addressing Seyd. "In accordance with the foolish custom that aims to make poor foreigners out of good Mexicans I received my education at a boarding-school in the city of Manchester, England."

Manchester, England! Center of the Lancashire cotton trade, inner shrine of commerce! Commercial essence exuded from the very name; it smelled to heaven of tin and rosin. Imagination faltered, nay, refused even to attempt to establish a relation between its prosiness and this romantic figure with a face cast in the image of the stone gods! Above all, a Manchester boarding-school! Seyd almost gasped. For to his knowledge of "fags" and "bullies," "form rows," "cribs and crams," and education by external application, gained by the perusal of *Tom Brown's School Days*, he had added the later, savagely impish realism of Kipling's *Stalky.*

And he knew what a living hell the life must have been to a high-strung Mexican youth. "Well!" he breathed at last. "I don't envy you the experience. I'm told that the English schoolboy isn't particularly sensitive or nice in his— his treatment of—"

"—Half-castes. Don't avoid the word. We Mexicans are proud of our Aztec blood. They did not love me, but I tell you, señor, that their dislike for me was as milk to fire compared with mine for them, and they left me alone after a couple had felt my knife. How I hated them—the conceited lackeys of masters as much as the bullocks of boys and their ox-like fathers. How they lectured me, the lackeys, for my 'cowardice' in using a knife—the cowardice of one small boy pitted against a hundred impish devils. But they were never able to blind me with their fustian ideals. Even then I could see through their sham morality, hypocritical humanity, insufferable conceit.

"'England is the workshop of the world!' They dinned it into us. In furtherance of the ideal they fouled the air with coal smoke, herded their men and women from the open farms into slums and brothels, and as they have done by their own so would they like to do for the world—make it one huge factory set in a slum." He had spoken all through with great heat. Glancing for the first time at Billy, he finished, more quietly, "That is why I do not speak English—because I hate both them and their tongue."

Now Billy's conception of John Bull and his island had been principally formed on the perfervid "tail-twisting" of the common-school histories, and Seyd, whose views had been corrected by wider reading, had to smile at his emphatic indorsement. "I'm with you. No English, please, in mine."

Even Sebastien smiled. "No, you are American—from our viewpoint, much worse. Just as sordid as the stupid English, you are quicker-witted, therefore more to be feared, and you stand forever at our gates, ready to force your commerce and ideas upon us. But much as we hate you, loath as we are to have you come among us, I would still have you to believe that this business was accidental. I, at least, did not plan your death."

"Then you do not speak for them?" Seyd glanced at the muleteers, now crouching over a second small fire they had built for themselves.

"*Quien sabe?*" Sebastien shrugged his shoulders. "They would think little of it. But what can you do? You have no proof. And I will see to it that they play you no more tricks."

Walking over, he kicked first one, then the other, in the small of the back. "Up, swine!" And while they stood shivering before them he gave them their orders—first to recover the baggage, then to convey the señors in safety to their mine. "Fail me in one thing," he concluded, with a frightful threat, "and I will pluck out your eyes and turn you out on the road."

Turning his back on them, he walked over to the horses, and had mounted before Seyd realized his intent. "You are not going?" he asked.

"Yes, it is only five leagues back to the hacienda where I left my own horse."

"First let me thank you."

Not seeing the touch of the spur that had caused the beast to rear suddenly, he imagined it shied at his outstretched hand. While curbing its plungings the other answered: "It is nothing. You owe me nothing. I came to repair a mistake and arrived too late. *Adios!*" And swinging the fighting beast out of the firelight into the dusk he galloped off, leaving Seyd standing with hand outstretched.

Returning to the fire, he passed close to the muleteers, whose faces, looking after him, expressed a curious mixture of dislike, suspicion, fear. Observing it, Billy laughed. "Our friend's football practice over there rather inclines me to favor his theories. I've seen a few walking-delegates in my time that I'd like to place under him. I'll bet you there are no labor troubles in his cosmos. Fancy a system that trains men to put your enemies away without so much as a wink. I call it ideal."

"Yes." Seyd laughed. "I have so much respect for it that I propose to keep watch and watch on the off chance of an attempt on our throats. If you'll just settle down for a snooze I'll take the first trick."

His laughter, however, covered feeling that had been deeply stirred by the events of the day. After Billy had curled up close to the fire his glance went over to the muleteers, who lay, heads muffled in their scarlet serapes, beside their own fire. Their very quiet stimulated thoughts which passed back through the medievalism of the "conquest" and the savagery of the Aztecs to the dim time that saw the erection of the temple they had passed that day. Stimulated by the distant roar of waters, the complaint of the wind in the trees, and the voices of night that rose out of the valley's black void, his fancies grew and possessed him until he saw his own civilization as a flash in the dark space of the ages. So absorbed was he that Billy's interruption came as a surprise.

"I've slept four hours. Time for your snooze."

CHAPTER V

"

Phe-ew!" Looking up from a treatise on bricklaying as applied to the building of furnaces, Billy pitched a stone at Seyd, who was experimenting with a batch of lime fresh drawn from a kiln of their own burning. "I'd always imagined bricklaying to be a mere matter of plumb and trowel, but this darned craft has more crinkles to it than the differential calculus. This fellow makes me dizzy with his talk of ties and courses, flues, draughts, cornering, slopes, and arches."

Leaning on his hoe, Seyd wiped his wet brow. "I'm finding out a few things myself. I'd always sort of envied a hod-carrier. But now I know that the humble 'mort' puts more foot-pounds of energy into his work than the average horse. As a remedy for dizziness caused by overstudy, mixing mortar has no equal. Come and spell me with this hoe."

"'And the last state of that man was worse than the first,'" Billy groaned. "*Can't* we hire a single solitary peon, Seyd?"

More eloquently than words, Seyd's shrug testified to the sullen boycott which had been maintained against them for the past three weeks. On the morning of their arrival at the mine, while the fear of Sebastien Rocha still lay heavy upon him, Carlos had been half bullied, half persuaded into the sale of Paz and Luz at a price which raised him almost to the status of a ranchero. But that single transaction summed up their dealings with the natives. No man had answered their call for laborers at wages which must have appeared as wealth to a peon. The charcoal-burners who drove their burros past the mine every day returned to their greetings either muttered curses or black stares. They were as stubborn in their cold obstinacy as the face of the temple god. Indeed, in these days the stony face of the image had become inseparably associated in Seyd's mind with the determined opposition that had routed his predecessors and now aimed to oust him. He saw it even in the soft, round faces of the children who peeped at him from the doorways of cane huts, a somber look, centuries old in its stubborn dullness.

Not that he and Billy were in the least discouraged. Once convinced that labor was not to be obtained, they had stripped and pitched in. In one month they rebuilt the adobe dwelling which had been somewhat shattered by the Dutchman's hurried exit, dug a lime kiln, and hauled the wood and stone for the first burning. They had completed the laying out of the smelter foundation, filling in odd moments by picking for the first charge the choicest ore from the hundreds of tons that the Englishmen had unwisely mined before they ran head-on into the hostile combination of freights and prices.

This last had been an inspiriting labor, for so rich were the values which the ore carried that after a trial assay Billy had danced all over the place beating an old pan. It is doubtful whether young men ever had better prospects; and so, knowing that Billy's present pessimism arose from a strong disinclination for physical labor in the hot sun, Seyd merely grinned. Sitting down on a pile of brick, he mopped his face and stared out over the valley.

Situated, as the mine was, on a wide bench which gave pause to the earth's dizzy plunge from the rim three thousand feet above, Seyd sat at the meeting-place of temperate and tropic zones. A hundred feet below—just where they had climbed the stiff trail out of the jungle that flooded the valley with its fecund life—a group of cocoanut palms stood disputing the downward rush of the pine, and all along the bench piñon and copal, upland growths, shouldered cedars and ceibas, the tropical giants. While these battled above for light and room there came, writhing snake-like up from the tropics, creepers and climbers, vines and twining plants, to engage the ferns and bracken, the pine's green allies. A plague of orchids here attacked the copal, wreathing trunk and limb in sickly flame. The bracken there overswept the riotous tropical life. All along the borderland the battle raged, here following a charge of the pine down a cool ravine, there mounting with the tropic growths to a sunlit slope. But in the valley below the tropics ruled clear down to the brilliant green of the San Nicolas cane fields.

"By the way"—Seyd spoke as his eye fell on these—"Don Luis is back from Mexico City. The hunchbacked charcoal-burner told me as he went past this morning."

"The deuce he did!" Of all the black looks that came their way that of the cripple was the most vindictive. "You must have him hypnotized."

"You wouldn't think so if you had heard his accent. 'El General is again at San Nicolas,' just as though he were sentencing me to hang. Nevertheless, the news comes pat. I think it would be good policy for me to run down and pay the denunciation taxes before we begin work on the smelter. No, I don't apprehend any trouble. Your Mexican hasn't much stomach for litigation, and no doubt the old fellow feels quite safe in his pull with the metals companies and railroads. But while he is still in the mind we had better pay the money and complete title. If he once gets wind of the smelter—"

"Just so." Billy threw down the hoe. "While you dress I'll saddle up a mule— if you will please say to which demon you prefer to intrust your precious neck. Light began the day by kicking me through the side of the stable. She needs chastening. But then Peace dined on my arm yesterday. It's Peace for yours, and I only hope you get it."

"Hum!" he coughed when, half an hour later, Seyd emerged shaved, bathed, and clad in immaculate white. "Is this magnificence altogether for el General, or did Caliban drop some word of our niece? Really, old chap, you look fine. If I were the señorita I'd go for you myself."

Though Seyd laughed, yet the instant he passed out of sight he fell into frowning thought which was evidently related to the letter he pulled out and reread while he rode down the steep grades. Written in a characterless round hand, it covered so many pages that he was halfway down before, after tearing it in shreds, he tossed it to the winds. Its destruction, however, did not seem to change his mood. He let Peace take her own way until, having slipped, slid, and tobogganed on tense haunches down the last grade, she felt able to assert her individuality by attempting to rub him off against a tree. Next she attempted the immolation of a fat brown baby that was rolling with a nest of young pigs in the dust outside a hut; and thereafter her performances were so varied that he was simply compelled to take some notice of the sights and sounds of the trail.

Not the least remarkable were the frequent and familiar scowls of the people he met. Various in expression, they ranged between the copious curses of the fat señora whose pacing-mule was driven by Peace off the trail, and the snarling malice of occasional muleteers; but, undisturbed, he pursued his inquiries for laborers at every chance.

"No, señor, we do not desire work."

The stereotyped answer merely stimulated the quiet persistence which formed the basis of his character, and he continued to ask at the village which raised graceful palm roofs out of a jungle clearing, at the ranchos which now began to cover the valley with a green checker of maize fields, and at scattered huts, half hidden by the rich foliage of palms and bananas. It was while he was questioning a peon who was hulling rice with a wooden pole and churn arrangement that the subdued hostility broke out in open demonstration.

The trail here ran between a fence of split poles, which inclosed the peon's corn and frijoles, and the steep bank of a dry creek bed, so that only a few feet leeway was left for the train of burros which came trotting out of the jungle behind him. In single file they could have passed, but looking around he saw they were coming three abreast.

Had he chosen, there was time to make the end of the fence. But he had seen behind the train the sparkling, beady eyes of Caliban, the hunchback, and the dark grins of two of his fellows. Flushing with quick anger, he backed Peace against the fence, leaned forward over her neck, and slashed with his whip at the leading beasts. Checked by this, they would have fallen back to single file but for the whips behind that bit out hair and hide and drove them on in a huddled mass.

It seemed for a few seconds that he would be crushed. That he escaped injury was simply due to the hereditary hate between the mule and the ass which suddenly turned Peace into a raging fiend. While her chisel teeth slit ragged hides her other and busier end beat a devil's tattoo on resounding ribs and filled the air with flying charcoal. Yet even her demoniac energies had their limitations. If she held the ground for herself and master she could not preserve the inviolability of his white trousers, which emerged sadly smudged from the fray. It is a pity she could not. Little things always cause the greatest trouble, and but for the smudges the incident would probably have closed with Seyd's challenge:

"Can't you be content with half the road?"

His patience even survived their insolent grins. Not until the hunchback in passing emitted a hoarse chuckle as he surveyed the smudges did Seyd's temper burst its bonds. Swinging his whip then with all his might, he laid it across the crooked shoulders once, twice, thrice, before the fellow sprang, snarling, out of reach. The others, who had already passed, came leaping back at his cry, knives flashing as they ran, and though they stopped under the sudden frown of a Colt's automatic, they did not retire, but stood, fingering their knives, muttering curses.

A little sorry on his part for the anger which had turned the sullen hostility into open feud, Seyd faced them, puzzled just what to do. It was too late to give way, for that would expose him to future insult. Yet if, taking the initiative, he should happen to kill a man, he knew enough of the quality of justice as dealt out by the Mexican courts to realize the danger.

While he debated, the puzzle was almost solved by the peon rice-huller, who came stealing up from behind the fence. Not until the man had swung his heavy pestle and was tiptoeing to his blow did Seyd divine the reason for the glances that were passing behind him. Looking quickly, he caught the glint of polished hardwood in the tail of his eye; then, without a pause for thought, he dropped flat on the rump of the mule, and not a second too soon, for, raising the hair on his brow as it passed, the club smashed down through the top rail of the fence. In falling backward his weight on the bridle brought Peace scurrying a few paces to the rear. When he snapped upright again the fourth enemy was also under his gun.

But what to do? The puzzle still remained—to be solved by another, for just then came a sudden beat of hoofs, and from behind a bamboo thicket galloped first the Siberian wolf hound, then the girl he had met at the train.

CHAPTER VI

So silently did the girl come that the charcoal-burners were forced to jump aside, and, springing in the wrong direction, the hunchback was bowled over by the beast of the *mozo* who rode at her back.

"Why, señor!" she exclaimed, reining in. Then taking in the knives, pistol, broken club, she asked, "They attacked you? Tomas!"

Her Spanish was too rapid for Seyd's ear, but it was easy to gather its tenor from the results. With a certain complaisance Seyd looked on while his enemies scattered on a run that was diversified by uncouth leaps as the *mozo's* whip bit on tender places.

"He struck at you?" She broke in on the rice-huller's voluble plea that never, *never* would he have raised a finger against the señor had he known him for a friend of hers! "Then he, too, shall be flogged."

"I would not wish—" Seyd began.

But she interrupted him: "You were going toward San Nicolas? Then I shall turn and ride with you." Anticipating his protest, she added, "I had already ridden beyond my usual distance."

Very willingly he fell in at her side, and they rode on till they met the *mozo* returning, hot and flushed, from the pursuit. He was keen as a blooded hound; it required only her backward nod to send him darting along the trail, and just about the time they overtook the charcoal-burners a sudden yelling in their rear told that the account of the rice-huller was in course of settlement.

Passing his late enemies, Seyd could not but wonder at their transformation. With the exception of the hunchback, in whose beady eyes still lurked subdued ferocity, all were sobbing, and even he broke into deprecatory whinings. Having read his Prescott, Seyd knew something of the rigid Aztec caste systems from which Mexican peonage was derived. Now, viewing their abjectness, he was able to apprehend, almost with the vividness of experience, the ages of unspeakable cruelty that had given birth to their fear. But that which astonished him still more was the indifference with which the girl had ordered the flogging.

Such glimpses of her face as he was able to steal while they rode did not aid him much. It was impossible to imagine anything more typically modern than the delicately chiseled features lit with a vivid intelligence which seemed to pulse and glow in the soft shadow beneath her hat. And when from her face his glance fell to her smart riding-suit of tan linen he was completely at sea.

Curiosity dictated his comment: "Your justice is certainly swift. Really I am afraid that I was the aggressor. At least I struck first."

"But not without cause." She glanced at his smudged clothes. "Tell me about it." And when he had finished she commented: "Just as I thought. And these are dangerous men. They would have killed you without a qualm. In the days that Don Sebastien was clearing the country of bandits he counted that hunchback one of his best men."

"Yet he whined like a puppy under your man's whip."

Smiling at his wonder, she went on to state the very terms of his puzzle. "You do not know them—the combination of ferocity and subservience that goes with their blood. In the old days he who raised his hand against the superior caste was put to death by torture, and, though, thank God, those wicked days are past, the effect remains. They are obedient, usually, as trained hounds, but just as dangerous to a stranger. If I had not ordered them flogged they would have taken it as license to kill you at their leisure."

"Now I realize the depth of my obligation."

He spoke a little dryly, and she leaped to his meaning with a quickness that greatly advanced her in his secret classification. "I have hurt your pride. You will pardon me. I had forgotten the unconquerable valor of the gringos."

"Oh, come!" he pleaded.

She stopped laughing. "Really, I did not doubt your courage. But do not imagine for one moment that they would attack you again in the open. A knife in the dark, a shot from a bush, that is their method, and if you should happen to kill one, even in self defense, gringos are not so well beloved in Guerrero but that some one would be found to swear it a murder. Be advised, and go carefully."

"I surely will." He was going on to thank her when she cut him off with the usual "It is nothing." Whereupon, respect for her intuition was added to the classification which was beginning to bewilder him by its scope and variety.

In fact, he could not look her way nor could she speak without some physical trait or mental quality being added to the catalogue. Now it was the quivering sensitiveness of her mouth, an unsuspected archness, the astonishing range of feeling revealed by her large dark eyes. Looking down upon the charcoal-burners, they had gleamed like black diamonds; in talking, their soft glow waxed and waned. Sometimes—but this was omitted from the classification because it only occurred when his head was turned—a merry twinkle illumined a furtive smile. Taken in all its play and sparkle, her face expressed a lively sensibility altogether foreign to his experience of women.

After a short silence she took up the subject again. "But I am giving you a terrible impression of our people. It is only in moments of passion that the old Aztec crops out. At other times they are kind, pleasant, generous. Neither are we the cruel taskmasters that some foreign books and papers portray us. You would not believe how angry they make me—the angrier because I have a strain of your blood in my own veins. My grandfather, you know, was Irish. It was from him I learned your speech."

The last bit of information was almost superfluous, for from no other source could she have obtained the pure lilting quality that makes the Dublin speech the finest English in the world. To it she had added an individual charm, the measured cadence and soft accent of her native Spanish, delivered in a low contralto that had in it a little break. Her laugh punctuated its flow as she came to her conclusion.

"But you will soon be able to see for yourself what terrible people we are."

He obtained one glimpse within the next mile. He had already noted the passing of the last wild jungle. From fields of maize which alternated with sunburned fields of *maguey* they now rode into an avenue that led on through green cane. Rising far above their heads, the cane marched with them for a half mile, then suddenly opened out around a primitive wooden sugar mill. Under the thatched roof of an open hut half-nude women were stirring boiling syrup in open pans, and at the sight of Francesca one of them came running out to the trail.

"Her baby is to be christened next Sunday," the girl told him as they rode on. "She was breaking her heart because she had no robe. But now she is happy, for I have promised to ask the good *mama* to lend her mine, which she has treasured all these years."

Soon afterward as they turned out of the cane into a new planting they almost ran down her uncle, who had come out to inspect the work. Only his quick use of the spur averted a collision, and as his own spirited roan sprang sideways Seyd noted with admiration that despite his bulk and age horse and man moved as one. If surprised at the sight of his niece in such company, the old man did not reveal it by so much as the lift of a brow. It was difficult even to perceive the twinkle in his eyes that lightened his chiding.

"*Ola*, Francesca! If there be no respect for thy own pretty neck, at least have pity on my old bones. It is you, señor? Welcome to San Nicolas."

Neither did Seyd's explanation of his business abate his brown impassivity. If assumed, his ponderous effort at recollection was wonderfully realistic.

"Ah, sí! Santa Gertrudis? If I remember aright, it was denounced before. Yes, yes, by several—but they had no good fortune. Still, you may fare better. Paulo, the administrador, will attend to the business."

With a wave of the hand, courteous in its very indifference, he put the matter out of his province and displayed no further interest until the girl told of the attack on Seyd. Then he glanced up quickly from under frowning brows.

"You had them whipped? *Bueno!* The rascals must be taught not to molest travelers. And now we shall ride on that the señor may break his fast. And thou, too, wicked one, will be late. As thou knowest, it is the only fault the good mother sees in thee."

"Would that it totaled my sins," she laughed. "To escape another black mark I shall have to gallop. *Ola!* for a race!"

As from a light touch of the spur her beast launched out and away, the roan reared and tried to follow, and while he curbed it back to a walk the old man's heavy face lit up with pleasure. "She rides well. I have not a vaquero with a better seat. But go thou, Tomas, lest she come to a harm. And you, señor, will follow?"

With a vivid picture of the figure Peace would cut in a race occupying the forefront of his mind it did not take Seyd long to choose. After the girl had passed from sight behind a clump of tamarinds he took note, as they rode along, of the peons who were laying the field out in shallow ditches wherein others were planting long shoots of seed cane. To his practical engineer's eye the hand-digging seemed so slow and laborious that he could not refrain from a comment.

"It seems to me that a good steel plow would do the work much cheaper."

"Cheaper? Perhaps." After a heavy pause, during which he took secret note of Seyd out of the corner of his eye, the old man went on: "To do a thing at less cost in labor and time seems to be the only thing that you Yankees consider. But cheapness is sometimes dearly purchased. Come! Suppose that I put myself under the seven devils of haste that continually drive you. What would become of these, my people? Who would employ them? It is true that theirs is not a great wage—perhaps, after all, totals less than the cost of your steel plow and a capable man to run it. We pay only three and a half cents for each ditch, in our currency, and a man must dig twelve a day. If he digs less he gets nothing.

"That does not seem just to you?" He read Seyd's surprise. "It would if you knew them. Grown children without responsibility or sense of duty are they. If left free to come and go, they would dig one, two, three ditches, enough and no more than would supply them with *cigarros* and *aguardiente*, and our work would never be done. As it is, they dig the full twelve, and have money for other necessities.

"The wage seems small?" Again he read Seyd's mind. "Yet it is all that we can afford, nor does it have to cover the cost of living. Each man has his patch of maize and frijoles, and a run for his chickens and pigs. Then the river teems with fish, the jungle with small game. His wage goes only for drink and *cigarros*, or, if there be sufficient left over, to buy a dress for his woman. They are perfectly content." Slightly lifting his heavy brows, he finished, looking straight at Seyd: "I am an old Mexican hacendado, yet I have traveled in your country and Europe. Tell me, señor, can as much be said of your poor?"

Now, in preparing a thesis for one of his social-science courses, Seyd had studied the wage scale of the cotton industry, and so knew that, ridiculously small as this peon wage appeared at the first glance, it actually exceeded that paid to women and children in Southern cotton factories. In their case, moreover, the pittance had to meet every expense.

He did not hesitate to answer. "I should say that your peons were better off, providing the conditions, as you state them, are general."

"And they are, señor, except in the south tropics, where any kind of labor is murder. But here? It is as you see; and why disturb it by the introduction of Yankee methods?"

Pausing, he looked again at Seyd, and whether through secret pleasure at his concession or because he merely enjoyed the pleasure of speaking out that which would have been dangerous if let fall in the presence of a countryman, he presently went on: "Therefore it is that I do not stand with Porfirio Diaz in his commercial policies. He is a great man. Who should know it better than I that fought with or against him in a dozen campaigns. And he has given us peace—thirty years of slow, warm peace. Yet sometimes I question its value. In the old time, to be sure, we cut each other's throats on occasion. In the mean time we were warmer friends. And war prevented the land from being swamped by the millions that overrun your older countries, the teeming millions that will presently swarm like the locusts over your own United States. As I say, señor, I am only an old Mexican hacendado, but I have looked upon it all and seen that where war breeds men, civilization produces only mice. If I be allowed my choice give me the bright sword of war in preference to the starvation and pestilence that thins out your poor."

Concluding, he looked down, interrogatively, as though expecting a contradiction. But though, after all, his argument was merely a restatement of the time-worn Malthusianism, coming out of the mouth of one who had strenuously applied it during forty years of internecine war, it carried force. Maintaining silence, Seyd stole occasional glances at the massive brown face and the heavy figure moving in stately rhythm with the slow trot of his horse, while his memory flashed over tale after tale that Peters, the station agent, had told him when he was out the other day to the railroad—tales of bravery, hardy adventures, all performed amidst the inconceivable cruelties of the revolutionary wars. Even had he been certain that the eventual peopling of the earth's vacant places would not force a return to at least a revised Malthusianism, it was not for his youth to match theories with age. When he did speak it was on another subject.

"I have been riding all morning on your land. I suppose it extends as far in the other direction?"

"A trifle." A deprecatory wave of the strong brown hand lent emphasis to the phrase. "A trifle, señor, by comparison with the original grant to our ancestor from Cortes. 'From the rim of the Barranca de Guerrero on both sides, and as far up and down from a given point as a man may ride in a day,' so the deed ran. Being shrewd as he was valiant, my forefather had his Indians blaze a trail in both directions before he essayed the running. A hundred and fifty miles he made of it when he started—not bad riding without a trail. But it is mostly gone by family division, or it has been forfeited by those who threw in their luck on the wrong side of a revolution. Now is there left only a paltry hundred or so thousands of acres—and this!"

For the first time pronounced feeling made itself felt through his massive reserve, and looking over the view that had suddenly opened, Seyd did not wonder at the note of pride. After leaving the cane they had plunged through green skirts of willow to the river that split the wide valley in equal halves, and from the shallow ford they now rode out on a grassy plateau that ran for miles along low lateral hills. Dotted with tamarinds, banyans, and the tall ceibas which held huge leafy umbrellas over panting cattle, it formed a perfect foreground for the hacienda, whose chrome-yellow buildings lay like a band of sunlight along the foot of the hill. The thick adobe walls that bound stables, cottages, and outbuildings into a great square gave the impression of a fortified town, castled by the house, which rose tier on tier up the face of the hill.

When they rode through the great gateway of the lower courtyard the interior view proved equally arresting. Mounting after Don Luis up successive flights of stone steps, they came to the upper courtyard, wherein was concentrated every element of tropical beauty—wide corridors, massive chrome pillars, time-stained arches, luxurious foliage. From the tiled roof above a vine poured in cataracts of living green so dense that only vigorous pruning had kept it from shutting off all light from the rooms behind. Left alone, it would quickly have smothered out the palms, orchids, rare tropical plants that made of the courtyard a vivid garden.

"They call it the *sin verguenza*." While he was admiring the creeper Francesca had joined them from behind. "Shameless, you know, for it climbs 'upstairs, downstairs,' nor respects even the privacy of 'my lady's chamber.' Thanks to the good legs of my beast, I escaped a scolding. Sit here where the vines do not obstruct the view."

If Seyd had been told a few minutes before that anything could have become her more than the tan riding-suit he would have refused to believe. But now by the evidence of his own eyes he was forced to admit the added charm of a simple batiste, whose fluffy whiteness accentuated her girlishness. The mad gallop had toned her usual clear pallor with a touch of color, and as she looked down, pinning a flower on her breast, he noted the perfect curve of her head.

"Room for a good brain there," he thought, while answering her observation. "It is beautiful. But don't you find it a little dull here—after Mexico City?"

"No." She shook her head with vigor. "Of course, I like the balls and parties, yet I am always glad to return to my horses and dogs and—though it is wicked to put them in the same category—my babies. There are always at least three mothers impatiently awaiting my return to consult me upon names. I am godmother to no less than seven small Francescas."

"I never should have thought it. You must have begun—"

"—Very young? Yes, I was only fifteen, so my first godchild is now seven. That reminds me—she is waiting below to repeat her catechism. There is just time—if you would like it."

"I would be delighted. So the position is not without its duties?"

"I should think not." Her eyes lit with a touch of indignation. "I hold the baby at the christening after helping to make the robe. When they are big enough I teach them their catechism. You could not imagine the weight of my responsibilities, and I believe that I am much more concerned for their behavior than their mothers. If any of them were to do anything really wicked"—her little shudder was genuine—"I should feel dreadfully ashamed. But they are really very good—as you shall judge for yourself. Francesca!" As, with a soft patter of chubby feet, a small girl emerged from a far corner, she added with archness that was chastened by real concern, "Now you must not dare to say that she isn't perfect."

In one sense the caution was needed. After a brave answer to the question "Who is thy Creator, Francesca?" the child displayed a slight uncertainty as to the origin of light, added a week or two to the "days of creation," and became hopelessly mixed as to the specific quantities of the "Trinity"—wherein, after all, she was no worse than the theologians who have burned each other up, in both senses, in furious disputes over the same question. But better, far better than letter perfection, was the simple awe of the small brown face and the devotion of the lisping voice which followed the tutor's gentle prompting.

"Fine! fine!" Seyd applauded a last valorous attack on the Ten Commandments, and the small scholar ran off clutching a silver coin, just so much the richer for his heretical presence. As he rose to follow his hostess inside he added, "If all the Francescas are equal to sample, the next generation of San Nicolas husbands will undoubtedly rise up and call you blessed."

"Now you are laughing at me," she protested. "Though that might be truly said of my mother. She is a saint for good works. But come, or I shall yet earn my scolding. And let me warn you to take care of your heart. All of the *caballeros* fall in love with mother."

It was quite believable. While seated in the dining-room, a vaulted chamber cool as a crypt in spite of the sunblaze outside, a room which would have seated an army of retainers, he observed the señora with the satisfaction that even a stranger may feel in the promise a handsome mother holds out to her girls. In addition to the sweetness of her eyes and her tenderly tranquil expression she had retained her youthful contour. She exhibited the miracle of middle age achieved without fat or stiffness. In her scarf and black lace she was maturely beautiful. Waving away his apologies for the intrusion, she was anxiously solicitous for his wants through the meal. Yet he noticed that in taking his leave an hour later she did not ask him to call again.

Up to that moment there had been no further mention of his business. But as he stood hesitating, loath to introduce it, Don Luis relieved his embarrassment. "Now you would see the administrador? I am sorry, señor, but it seems that he is away at Chilpancin about the sale of cattle. But if you will intrust your moneys to Francesca she will see to the business and have the papers sent out to the mine."

Neither did Francesca, when saying good-by, ask him to return. But, conscious that with all their kind hospitality they still regarded him as an intruder, Seyd was neither offended nor surprised. He was even a little astonished when Don Luis stated his intention of riding with him as far as the cane.

Until they came to the ford they rode in silence. Though only a few inches deep at this season, the river's wide bed proclaimed it one of those torrential streams which rise from a trickle to a flood in very few hours, and when he remarked upon it Don Luis assented with his heavy nod.

"*Si*, it is very treacherous. One night during the last rains it rose fifty feet and swept down the valley miles wide, bearing on its yellow bosom cattle, houses, sheep, and pigs, and it drowned not a few of our people. And each year the floods go higher. Why? Because of the cursed lust that would mint the whole world into dollars. Year by year your Yankee companies are stripping the pine from the upper valley, and, though I have spoken with Porfirio Diaz about it, he is mad for commerce. He would see the whole state of Guerrero submerged before he revoked one charter. And they even try to make me a party to it. 'General, if you will grant us a concession to do this, that, the other? If you will only allow us to run a branch line into your pine we can make big money—guarantee you half a million pesos.' When I am in Mexico your Yankee promoters swarm round me like hungry dogs. But never have I listened, nor ever will!"

He struck the pommel of his saddle a heavy blow, then looked his surprise as Seyd spoke. "I should not think that you would. I understand your feelings."

"You do? *Caramba!* Then you are the first Yankee that ever did. In return for your sympathy let me offer you advice. You are not the first man to denounce on my land, nor is Santa Gertrudis the only location. Yankees, English, French, Germans, they have come, denounced claims here and there, but no man has ever held one. No man ever *will*. Already you have tasted the bitter hostility of my people, and were I to nod not even the American Ambassador could save you alive. And this is only the beginning. Let me return your money? Mexico is one great mine. Anywhere you can kick the soil and uncover a fortune."

"But none like the Santa Gertrudis." Seyd smiled. "Of course, I feel it's pretty raw for me to force in on your land; but, knowing that if I don't some other will, I shall have to refuse. As for the opposition—that is all in the day's work." He finished, offering his hand. "But I hope this won't prevent us from being good neighbors?"

Shaking his massive head, Don Luis reined in his horse. "No, señor, we can never be that. But next to a good friend I count a hearty enemy, and you may depend upon me for that."

With a courteous wave of the hand he rode off; and, watching him go at a stately canter, Seyd muttered, "Enemy or friend, you are a fine old chap."

"You are surely a fine old chap."

Retracing his path through the long succession of farm, jungle, and fields, Seyd repeated it, and as he rode along he saw things in a new light. As he passed through one village at sundown the entire population was filing into church, the peons in clean blankets, their women in decent black. The next hamlet was in the throes of a fiesta. Girls in white, garlanded with flaming flowers, were dancing the eternal jig of the country with their brown swains. And these two functions, church and *baile*, marked the bounds of their simple life. A plenty of rice and frijoles, a peso or two for clothing, were all that they asked or needed.

While prospecting in the Sierra Madres Seyd had drawn many a comparison between the happy indolence of the peon and the worry, strain, strife to live up to a standard just beyond income that obtains in American life. Because the peon had time to think his simple thoughts, listen to bird song and the music of babbling streams, to watch the splendors of sunrise and sunset over purple valleys, Seyd's suffrage had often gone to him. Observing this pastoral life in its tropical setting of palms and jungle, the opinion grew into a strong conviction.

"The old fellow's right!" he ejaculated, riding out of the last village into the jungle proper. "We have nothing to give his people, and we'd surely kill all they have."

Though the profusion of foliage which made of the trail one long green tunnel prevented him from seeing it, he was now riding along at the foot of the Barranca wall. Its deep shadow already filled the jungle with a twilight that thickened into night as he rode. But, knowing that whatever her faults of temperament Peace could be trusted to fetch her own stable, he left her to take her own way while he pursued his thoughts. While the siren whistle of beetles, chatter of *chickicuillotes*—wild hens of the jungle—deafened his ears, he tried to bring the crowding impressions of the day into some kind of order—no easy task when a fire-eating old general and a typical Mexican mother had to be reconciled in thought with a young girl who possessed the face of a Celt, eyes of a Spaniard, vivacity of a Frenchwoman, and American intelligence.

Next he fell to speculating upon the causes which had kept her single at an age that, according to Mexican standards, placed her hopelessly upon the shelf, and he found the answer in the gossip of the American station agent on his last trip out to the railroad. "She could have had her cousin Sebastien any time, and there were others around these parts. But once let a high-strung girl like her get a glimpse of the outside world and no common hacendado can ever hope to tie her shoestring. They say she has had other chances— attachés of foreign legations in Mexico City. But she turned 'em down—I don't know why, unless it's ideals." With a humorous twinkle the agent had added: "Bad things, ideals—always in the way. If you happen to have any in stock give 'em to the first beggar you meet along the road. Hers are keeping San Nicolas and El Quiss from reuniting, but she don't seem to care."

"A fine girl—the man will be lucky that gets her." Seyd now re-expressed the agent's homely verdict. "If it wasn't—" He stopped short, with a savage laugh. "You darned fool! mooning over a girl who would turn up her pretty nose at any gringo, much more one that has forced himself in on her uncle's land. Your business is to get a fortune out of the mine, and do it quick. And even if it wasn't—"

The thought was never finished, for the last few minutes had brought him out into the starlight at the foot of the Barranca wall, and as Peace gathered herself for the scramble upward the jungle lit up with a sudden flash. Before Seyd's ears caught the report he felt his left shoulder clutched, as it were, by a red-hot hand. The next second he was almost thrown by the mule's sudden plunge—fortunately, for otherwise the bullet that came out of a second flash would have smashed through his brain.

"Muzzle-loaders!" In the moment he lay on the mule's neck he divined it from the thick explosion. Then the thought, "It will take them a minute to reload," followed a quick calculation, "They'll catch me again on the first turn."

With him action always sprang of subconscious processes which were quicker than thought, and while he crouched on her neck and Peace took the turn on a scrambling gallop he turned loose with both of his Colts, aiming at the spot from which the flashes had come. And the sequel proved his judgment. This time a single flash announced the bullet which grazed the mule's rump just as she shot into a patch of woodland.

"Reckon I made one of you sick," he interpreted the single shot.

The burning smart of his wound and the treachery of the attack had loosed within him a fury of anger. Reining in, he felt his shoulder. The bullet had plowed a furrow in the flesh of the upper arm, but, muttering "I guess it's bled about all it's going to," he first tied the mule to a tree, then slid the "reloads" into his guns.

It would have been foolish to expose himself in the open trail under the clear starlight. Resisting the savage impulse which urged him to close quarters, he crawled back to the edge of the timber and again turned loose his guns, searching the jungle below with a swinging muzzle. Time and again he did it, thanking his stars whenever he reloaded for the forethought which had caused Billy to slip an extra box of cartridges into the holsters, and not until only one charge was left did he pause to listen.

Whether or no it was the firing that had frightened even the night birds into temporary quiet, not even a twig stirred in the darkness below. He caught only the distant whooping which told that Billy had heard, and as this drew nearer with astonishing quickness Seyd rose and went back to his mule.

"Coming downhill hell for leather!" he muttered. "If I don't hurry he'll break his neck."

CHAPTER VII

One afternoon about a week later Mr. William Thornton was to be seen mixing mortar for the bricks he was laying on the smelter foundation. Rising almost sheer from the edge of the bench behind him, the Barranca wall shut off the western breeze, and from its face the fierce sunblaze was reflected in quivering waves of heat. Coming out from an early lunch he had noted that the thermometer registered ninety in the shade, and he was now ready to swear that with one more degree he himself would be able to supply all the moisture required for the operation.

While working he cast occasional glances toward the house; and when, the mortar being mixed, he began to lay brick he used the trowel with care lest its clink should awaken Seyd. For though the blood loss from a severed artery had left him quite weak, he had obstinately refused to stop work. To-day he had even balked at the suggestion of a siesta until Billy had lain down himself. As soon as Seyd fell asleep Billy had slipped out, and when he now paused to listen the concern in his look passed into sudden attention as the clink of a shod hoof rose up from the trail below.

Five minutes passed before he heard it again, and in the mean time his actions bespoke an intelligent appreciation of the needs of the case. Picking up a Winchester which leaned against a tree, he crouched behind his bricks, and while training it on the point where the trail emerged on the bench a ferocious scowl overshadowed his sunburn.

"If we played it your way I'd brown you the second your nose shows," he muttered as the hoofbeats grew louder. "Thank your musty old saints that we don't. Ah! Eh? Well!"

The interjections respectively fitted the wolf hound, her young mistress, and the *mozo*, as they appeared in the order named. As only Billy's head showed over the bricks, and both were on the same color scheme, he was practically invisible; and, reining up her beast, the girl allowed her curious gaze to wander around the bench from the gaping hole where the drift ran into the vein over the adobe hut and foundation—just missing Billy's head—to the blue-green piles of copper ore.

"So this is the *mina!*" Her tone denoted disappointment. "Good heavens! Tomas, is this the wealth the gringos seek? What an ado over a pile of stones! I should think Don Luis would be thankful to have them carted away."

She had spoken in Spanish, but when, having shed his arsenal under cover of the bricks, Billy rose and came forward, she addressed him in English. "Mr. Thornton, is it not? We have brought the papers from the administrador—at least, Tomas has. I am playing truant. Though it is only

- 41 -

fifteen miles from here to San Nicolas, this is the first time that I have seen the place. Where is Mr. Seyd?"

Now than Billy, was there never a young man more naturally chivalrous. Usually a locomotive could not have dragged from him a single word calculated to shock or offend a girl. But in his confusion at finding an expected enemy changed into a charming friend he let slip the naked truth. "He was shot—returning from your place."

"Señor! He—he is not—dead?"

There was no mistaking her concern. Sorry for his abruptness, Billy plunged to reassure her. "No! no! Only wounded."

"Is he—much hurt?"

It occurred to Billy that a flesh wound was, after all, rather a small price for such solicitude. But where a touch of jealousy might have caused another to make light of Seyd's wound, his natural unselfishness made him paint it in darker colors. "The bullet cut an artery, and he's pretty weak from loss of blood. Yet he won't lay off. I had to trick him into a siesta to-day. I'll go call him."

But she raised a protesting hand. "No! no! Let him sleep. You can give him the papers. Tell him when he awakes that he will hear from us again."

With a smile which caused Billy additional regret for his lack of wounds she rode off at a pace which filled him with anxiety for her neck. Until he caught a glimpse of her, foreshortened to a dot on the trail far below, he stood watching. Then, muttering "I'll bet Seyd will raise Cain when he awakes," he went back to his work.

Nor was he mistaken, for when Seyd came out, yawning and stretching, an hour or so later, the last vestige of sleep was burned up by the sudden flash of his eyes. "You darned chump! Do we have visitors so often that you let me sleep on like a rotten log?"

Neither was he appeased by Billy's answer, delivered with an irritating grin: "Why should she wish to see you when I was around? A pallid wretch who has to make three tries to cast a shadow!"

"He has, has he?" Seyd growled. "Well, I'm solid enough to punch your fat head."

The atmosphere having thus been cleared, he commented: "Went off to tell the General, eh? I wonder how he'll take it?"

"Shouldn't imagine he'd shed any tears—unless at their poor shooting. Well, we'll see!"

And see they did, for as they sat at lunch on the second day thereafter a yell followed by the crack of a whip brought them out just in time to see Caliban, the charcoal-burner, and the peon rice-huller coming on a shuffling run ahead of Tomas. The bloody bandages which bound the head of one and the leg of the other testified to Seyd's shooting, just as their glazed eyes and painful pantings told of the merciless run ahead of the *mozo*. It required only the hempen halter which each wore around his neck to complete the picture of misery.

"These be they that attacked you, señor?" While the rice-huller squirmed under a sudden cut of his whip the *mozo* went on: "This son of a devil was found nursing a wound in his hut, and he told on the other. Don Luis sends them with his compliments to be hanged at your leisure. If it please you to have it done now—there is an excellent tree."

Too surprised to answer, Seyd and Billy stood staring at each other until, taking silence for consent, the *mozo* began to herd his charges toward the said tree. "Here!" Seyd called him back. "This is kind of Don Luis, and you will please convey to him our thanks. It is very thoughtful of you to pick out such a fine tree, but, while we are sure that they would look very nice upon it, it is not the habit with our people to hang save for a killing, and I, as you see, am alive."

The *mozo's* dark brows rose to the eaves of his hair. "But of what use, señor, to hang *after* the killing? Will the death of the murderer bring the murdered to life? But hang him in good season and you will have no murder. And this is a good tree, low, with strong, wide branches ordained for the purpose. See you! One throw of the rope, a pull, a knot—'tis done, easily as drinking, and they are out of your way."

It was good logic; but, while admitting it, Seyd still pleaded his foolish national custom.

Though his bent brows still protested against such squeamishness, the *mozo* politely submitted. "*Bueno!* it is for you to say. I leave them at your will to cure or kill."

"Now, what shall we do?" Seyd consulted Billy. "If we send them back the old Don will surely hang them."

"Well, what if he does? I'm sure that I don't care a whoop—" He paused, then suddenly exclaimed: "Are we crazy? Here we have been chasing labor all over the valley, and now that it is offered us free we turn up noses. Keep them, you bet! Put it into Spanish as quickly as you can."

Smiling, the *mozo* nodded comprehension. "As you say, señor, a live slave is better than a dead thief. They are at your orders to kill by rope or work."

Though it was scarcely his thought, Seyd allowed it to go at that. Throwing the ends of the halters to Billy, the *mozo* concluded his mission. "It remains only to say that Don Luis will have you come to San Nicolas till your wound is cured."

"Fine!" Billy enthusiastically commented, when the invitation was translated. "I've said all along that you ought to lay off. Go down for a week. By the time you come back I'll have these chaps beautifully broken."

"And you unable to speak a word of Spanish—not to mention the risk to your throat?" Seyd shook his head. "Besides, the old fellow made no bones of his feelings the other day. The invitation is merely in reparation for what he considers a violation of his hospitality. If it wasn't—My place is here."

Accordingly, the *mozo* carried back to San Nicolas a note which, if not penned in the best Spanish, yet caught its grave courtesy so cleverly that its perusal at the dinner table caused Francesca to pause and listen, drew an approving smile from the señora, and produced from Don Luis his heavy nod.

"The young man is a fine *caballero*. Your ordinary gringo would have saddled himself upon us for three months, and we should have been worn to skeletons by his parrot chatter. As he lets us off so easily, I must ride up to the mine and warn those rascals to play him no tricks."

Meanwhile Seyd and Billy had been giving the disposition of the said rascals considerable thought. After the *mozo* left, Billy cut the halters from around their necks and brought them food and drink from the house. But whether or no they considered this fair front as being assumed to emphasize future tortures the two kept their sullen silence.

"If we have to stand guard all the time we'd be better without them," Billy doubted.

"Yes," Seyd acquiesced. "Unless we can find some incentive. I wonder if they have families." When the two returned nods to his questions he continued, hopefully: "There we have it. Your Mexican peon takes homesickness worse than a Swiss. If we offer them a fair wage while the smelter is building I think they'll prove faithful. At least we can try."

To an experienced eye—the *mozo's*, for instance—the sudden brightening of the dark faces might have meant something else than relief. At first Caliban seemed to find the good news impossible. But presently, setting it down as another idiocy of the foolish gringos, his incredulity vanished. In one hour he and the rice-huller were transformed from sullen foes to eager servants.

Indeed, what with their willing work that afternoon and next morning, the smelter foundation had risen a full yard by the time that Don Luis came riding up to the bench.

Looking up from a blue print of the foundation, Seyd saw him coming at the heavy trot which combined military stiffness with vaquero ease, and noting the keen glance with which he swept the bench the thought flashed upon him, "Now the cat's out of the bag!" He did not, however, try to smuggle the animal in again. When, greetings over, Don Luis turned a curious eye on the foundation he answered the unspoken question. "A smelter, señor."

"A smelter?" For once the old fellow's massive self possession showed slight disturbance. "I thought—"

"That it took a fortune to build one." Seyd filled in his pause. "It does—to put in a modern plant." While he went on explaining that this was merely an old-style Welch furnace of small capacity he felt the constraint under the old man's quiet, and was thereby stimulated to a mischievous addition. "You see, the freight rates on crude ore from this point are prohibitive, but one can make good money by smelting it down into copper matte."

"A good plan, señor." Like a tremor on a brown pool, his disquiet passed. "And how long will it be in the building?"

"We had calculated on four months. But with the help you so kindly sent us we can do it now in two."

He could not altogether repress a mischievous twinkle. But Don Luis gave no sign. "*Bueno!* It was for this that I came—to read these rascals their lesson." Menacing the peons with a weighty forefinger, he went on: "Now, listen, *hombres!* Since it has pleased the señor to save you alive, see that you repay his mercy with faithful labor. If there be any failure, tricks, or night flittings, remember that there is never a rabbit hole in all Mexico but where Luis Garcia can find you."

Emphasizing the threat with another shake of his finger, he turned and went on with quiet indifference to comment upon the scenery. "A beautiful spot. Once I had thought to build here, but one cannot live on the edge of a cliff, and San Nicolas has its charm. Is it true that we cannot tempt you to come down? The señora begs that you reconsider."

But he nodded his appreciation of Seyd's reasons. "*Si, si,* a man's place is with his work—and I have stayed too long. There is business forward at Chilpancin, and even now I should be miles on the way."

"Will you not stay for lunch?" Seyd protested.

But replying that he had already lunched at a ranch in the valley, the old man rode away on his usual heavy lope. "You see," Seyd commented, watching him go, "it is all right for me to accept his invitation, but he will not eat of our bread."

"Well, I don't blame him," Billy answered. "I'd feel sore myself if I were he. But, say, we're getting quite gay up here. Regular social whirl. I wonder who's next? We only need mamma to complete the family."

The remark was prophetic, for, while the señora did not herself brave the Barranca steeps, only two days thereafter Francesca and the *mozo* reappeared driving before them a mule whose panniers were crammed with eggs and cheese, butter and honey, fruit, both fresh and preserved, also a full stock of bandages, liniments, curative simples, and home-made cordials. While unpacking them on the table in their house the girl laughingly explained that if Seyd would not come to be cured the cures must needs come to him.

"This is a wash for the wound." She patted a large fat jug. "This other is to be taken every hour. Of this liquor you must take a glass at bed-time. Those pills must be swallowed when you rise. This"—noting Billy's furtive grin, she finished with a laugh—"you will not have room for more. Give the rest to Mr. Thornton. But under pain of the good mamma's severest displeasure I am to see you drink at least two cups of this soup."

"You shall if you stay to lunch," Seyd said. "Billy makes gorgeous biscuit, and they'll go finely with the honey."

"If you can eat bacon—we have only that and a few canned things," Billy added, a little dubiously, and would have extended the list of shortcomings only that she broke in:

"Just what I like. I'm tired of Mexican cooking, and I am dreadfully hungry."

That this was no idle assertion she presently proved, and while she ate of their rough food with the appetite of perfect health their acquaintance progressed with the leaps and bounds natural to youth. Before the end of the meal she had drawn Billy completely out of his painful bashfulness, and he was telling her with great pride of his beautiful sister while she contemplated her photograph with head held delicately askew.

"Yes, she's fair," he told her, adding with great pride, "but not a bit like me."

"The most wonderful hair!" Seyd volunteered. "Darkest Titian above a skin of milk."

"Oh, you make me envious!" she cried, with real feeling. "I love red hair. Luisa Zuluaga, my schoolmate in Brussels, had it combined with great black Spanish eyes. She got her colors from an Irish great grandfather who came over a century ago to coin pesos for the Mexican mint. Now, why couldn't I have had them?"

Observing the fine-spun cloud that flew like a dark mist around the ivory face, Seyd could not find it in his heart to blame her grandfather, and, if good taste debarred him from saying it, the belief was nevertheless expressed through the permitted language of the eyes. Perhaps this accounted for the suddenness with which her long dark lashes swept down over certain mischievous lights.

Any but an expert in feminine psychology might indeed have found himself puzzled by certain phases of her manner. Its sympathy, addressing Billy, would give place to a slight reserve with Seyd, then this would melt and give place to unaffected friendliness. Occasionally, too, she offered all the witchery of her smiles, yet the hypothetical expert would never have suspected her of coquetry. The feeling was far too mischievous for the fencing of sex. Its key was to be found in the thought that passed in her mind. "'Almost pretty enough to marry,' you said. The trouble is that my girlish beauty is in inverse ratio to my future fatness. What a pity!"

Yet this little touch of pique was never sufficiently pronounced to interfere with her real enjoyment. As for them—it was a golden occasion. If they ate little, they still feasted their eyes on the face that bloomed like a rich flower in the soft shadows of the adobe hut, their ears on her low laughter and soft woman's speech. They found it hard to believe when she sprang up with a little cry: "I have been here two hours! Now I have earned my scolding. The *madre* only let me come under a solemn promise to be back before sunset."

Had they been unaware of the principal concomitant in the charm of the hour, knowledge would have been forced upon them when she rode away, for, though the birds still sang and the hot sun poured a flood of light and heat down on the bench, somehow things looked and felt cold and gray.

And she? Going downgrade an afterglow of smiles lent force to her murmur: "Gringos or no, they are very nice."

CHAPTER VIII

A hard gallop of eight miles carried Francesca to the forks where the path to and from Santa Gertrudis joined the main valley trail, and she had traveled no more than a hundred yards beyond before she was roused from renewed musings by the thud of hoofs. Turning in her saddle, she saw Sebastien coming along the valley trail at a gallop. Passing the *mozo*, whose beast had lagged, the hacendado pulled his beast down to a trot, and as Tomas, answering a question, nodded backward toward the hills, vexation swept the girl's face.

It cleared, however, as quickly, and while waiting for Sebastien she measured him with a narrow glance. The straight, lithe figure, easy carriage, dark, quiet face could stand inspection, and she paid unconscious tribute. "If I hadn't gone to Europe I suppose—" A decided shake of the head completed while dismissing the thought. In the next breath she murmured, "Now for a fight." Yet her expression, saluting him, displayed no apprehension.

"Yes, I was at Santa Gertrudis." She quietly answered his question. "Two of our people shot one of the gringos as he was leaving our place, and the good *mama* would have it that it was our duty to cure him."

"Ah! the good mother?" He raised his brows. "And she chose you for her doctor?"

"As you see."

"Yes, I see. 'No, Francesca, thou canst not go. It would not be right for a young girl—well, if you must—' I hear it as though I had been there, and wonder that the señora, who was brought up in the letter of our conventions, should send her daughter to a gringo camp with only a *mozo* for escort. But Don Luis? Is he also mad?"

"No, only wise." She answered with irritating simplicity. "Take care that you do not put heavier strains on a slight kinship. Third, fifth, tenth, just what is the degree of our cousinship?"

"God knows!" He shrugged. "The slighter the better. 'Twill serve till replaced by a closer."

"Which will be never."

"Only the gods say 'never.'" He quoted the proverb. "But returning to your *amigos*, the gringos—"

"My *amigos*?"

"You have received and repaid their visits. But listen! It is not that I would set bounds for your freedom, but if you had stood, as I have, on a street corner in Ciudad, Mexico, and had heard the gringo tourists pass comments on our women—*Dios!* I choke at the thought! If you but realized their coxcombry, conceit, the contempt in which they hold us—"

She had flushed slightly, but with a toss of her head she broke in: "It is not necessary. I have heard young Mexican men comment on both our own and American women. If the gringos can teach them any lessons—"

"Apes!" he burst angrily in. "Fools! The degenerate apes who put on the vices of civilization with its collars!"

"Perhaps. But, even so, it makes for the same point—there are gringos and gringos just as we have Mexicans *and* Mexicans."

"And these, of course, are the other sort?"

"Exactly!" She robbed his sarcasm by her quiet. "If one judges, as one must, by their behavior. I am pleased to find you, for once, of my opinion."

"Of your opinion?" He regarded her with sudden sternness. "That is, to be friends with these men who have forced themselves in on your lands? I had never expected to hear it fall from the lips of a Garcia. Now listen! What if your people did wound this man? Is he the first? Will he be the last?" His face darkening under a rush of blood, he continued: "I had thought this pair would soon ruin themselves as did the other fools before them. But since they are working on a surer plan—"

"What do you mean?" She searched his face.

"So anxious?" he laughed bitterly. "What is it to you?"

"Only that I would not have them murdered."

"And would they be the first? Is there a foot of Mexican soil which has not been soaked with good Mexican blood that you should be so careful for a gringo?" Slanting through an opening in the trees overhead the sun shone on his face, transforming it into a red mask of hate. "As yet no one of them has secured himself in the Barranca de Guerrero! So long as a Rocha is left to do the duty that belongs to the Garcias no one of them ever will."

But now he had touched another string, and, straightening in her saddle, she gave him look for look. "When the Garcias need the Rochas to settle their quarrels it will be time for you to interfere. I should not advise you to speak thus to my uncle."

Nevertheless she flinched a little at his answer. "That is my intention—this very night."

With that they rode on, in silence for a while, then speaking of other things. But when he left her in the upper courtyard an hour later she stood at her door, listening apprehensively to the jingle of his spurs along the gallery. When he took a chair beside Don Luis, who sat there smoking, she listened for a while. Then, flushing suddenly, she hastily went in.

If she had remained there was nothing to hear, for during many minutes the conversation ran altogether on the herds as they came winding in from distant pastures to the corrals in the square. Night had reduced everything to a dark blur before Sebastien commented on a yellow twinkle high up on the Barranca wall.

"That will be the gringos' light at Santa Gertrudis." After a long pause, "It is now a month past since they came, and—they are still here."

Don Luis flicked the ash from his cigar. "What hurry?"

"But this new business? The smelter you spoke of the other day."

"*Si*, the smelter?"

Sebastien gave his own interpretation to the other's slow tone. "Then there is something forward?"

"What need? The gringo at the station tells me they have no money. A single mistake and they are done." After a sententious pause he added, "It is the part of youth to make mistakes."

The dusk did not conceal the other's impatience. "But why this tender care? Are they so different from the others? A word from thee and—"

"Yes, yes, a nod and it would have been done long ago. There speaks young blood—the hot blood that lost us Texas and Alta California. These lads are of good family, Sebastien, and there can be no disappearance without inquiry. Their death would be but one more thorn in the side of the rabid beast that requires small urging to devour us. No, let them make their own end."

"And Francesca? Is she to have the run of their camp?"

Don Luis's deep laugh rumbled through the courtyard. "At last from a long cast we come to the quarry. Francesca? She is a wild filly, the despair of every staid tabby in the countryside. Long ago I discovered that the one way to manage her was to let her have her head. Nor will it be the part of wisdom for thee to interfere."

"Neither would I try—yet. Commands are for husbands; lovers must wait. That which I propose she will never know. It is—" Answering the other's interrogative look, he leaned over, whispering in rapid Spanish.

Don Luis emitted an amused chuckle. "Sebastien, thou art truly a devil. Had thy father possessed but the half of thy wit, some things had gone different in the last war. Yes, feet that are still spoiling good sod would now be rotten bones." After a pause he went on: "It seems a scurvy trick, yet it depends on the men themselves. But—if they rise not at the bait?"

"If?" Sebastien repeated it with bitter scorn. "Was there ever a gringo that would not bite at such? They are kind as goats. I ask only that you go there with Francesca at the close of the week."

"And thou?"

"I shall go there to-morrow."

CHAPTER IX

Living in the letter of his intention, Sebastien was up next morning and had covered ten miles of the trail before the sun rose over the Barranca wall. Early as it was, however, others were already abroad. The sudden increase in his family had obliged Seyd to make a journey out to the railroad for more provisions, and when Sebastien paused to breathe his beast halfway up the grade to the bench, a good glass would have shown him Light and Peace gingerly picking their way along the trail that had been built by Don Luis's orders around the slide on the opposite wall.

As usual, Sebastien's approach was announced by the ring of hoofs, but, imagining it to be some charcoal-burner, Billy, who was already at his bricks, did not look up till warned by Caliban's stealthy hiss. In his surprise he forgot to reply to Sebastien's greeting, and simply answered the other's question.

"Don Roberto? He is not here?"

"No, gone out to the railroad. Won't be back for three days."

"*Caramba!* After I had climbed these heights to see him!" Though his eyebrows and hands both testified to Sebastien's disappointment, a sharper eye than Billy's might have discerned the underlying satisfaction. Moreover, if he appeared merely inquisitively friendly during the hour he stayed to chat, not one minute was wasted. From the first question to his final comment on Billy's work, "You gringos are certainly a wonderful people," all was directed to one end.

"Yes, we usually get there," Billy modestly admitted, and his next words paved a lovely road for Sebastien to come to his purpose. "The building would go faster if I hadn't so many things to do. After laying bricks all day I have to turn in and cook, and, though it's pretty tough, there doesn't seem to be any way out of it. We tried both of the peons at the cooking and nearly died of the hash they served up."

"Tut! tut!" Sebastien was there with ready sympathy. "This is too bad. Soon you will be completely worn out." After a pause, during which he may be imagined as taking Billy's mental temperature, he said: "*Bueno!* I have it! I shall send you a cook—one than whom there is no finer in all this country."

If he had harbored any suspicions, Billy's beaming smile now wiped them out. "That's awfully good of you. Seyd will be ever so glad. When can we expect your cook?"

"To-morrow afternoon." Scenting hospitality in Billy's glance toward the hut, Sebastien hastily added, "That is, if I reach home to-night—to do which

I shall have to be going." And refusing the offer of lunch which justified his premonition, he rode away, leaving Billy puffed up with pride.

"I rather think I turned that trick well," he congratulated himself. "Seyd couldn't have done it a bit better." Occasional fat chuckles emitted during the afternoon testified to his increasing opinion of his own diplomacy. But his rising pride did not attain its meridian until, midway of the following afternoon, a pretty brown girl came driving a burro up the trail.

Having anticipated a man cook, it required five minutes of vehement Spanish, helped out by a wealth of gesticulation, to convince Billy that the girl was not an estray from a neighboring hamlet, and while her dark eyes, white teeth, and shapely brown arms were engaged in explanation they wrought other work. By the time Billy was finally able to understand the fact he was hardly in condition to pass upon it.

It is only right to state that he had little time for reflection, for from the very beginning the girl took the direction of affairs into her own hands. Driving her burro over to the stable she unpacked a stone *metate*, or grinding-stone, a pestle, and a quantity of soaked corn. She turned the beast out to graze, then dropped at once on her knees and began grinding paste for the supper tortillas, or cakes. When, toward evening, Billy dropped in for a drink he found her mantle spread on his bed and certain articles of feminine wear depending from the nails which had hitherto been sacred to his own clothing.

Blushing furiously, he went out—without the drink. But, though his colors would have done credit to a girl, they were not to be weighed in the same balance with the green peppers stuffed with minced beef that she served at supper with the tortillas. While eating with an appetite born of a protracted canned diet it is to be feared that he fed just as ravenously on the atmosphere shed by her luxurious presence. When, after supper, he sat in the doorway and watched the blood-reds of the sunset flow through the valley he might, with his fiery stubble, have passed for some ancient Celt at the mouth of his cave. Not until he caught a second glimpse of the mantle while stealing a look at the girl washing up dishes did he return to his usual bashful self. Slipping quietly inside, he gathered up the blankets off Seyd's bed and carried them out to make his own couch under a tree.

This procedure on his part the girl watched with a certain astonishment which she vented on Caliban while giving him his breakfast next day. "I had thought differently of the gringos. Be they all like this one—"

"Give time, give time!" the hunchback advised. "Big fish are ever slow at the hook, but when they once rise—" The tortilla he used for illustration vanished at one gulp. "Wait till thou seest Don Roberto. There's a man! Of his own strength he threw a burro off the trail into the Barranca and so turned the train that would otherwise have driven him and the 'Red Head' into the cañon. 'Tis so. The history of it was written by Don Sebastien's whip on the shoulders of Mattias and Carlos. And what of the magic that turned my bullet fired at twenty yards, then found me and Calixto in black jungle and shot us down from the high cliff? Si, chief of the other is he, so waste not thy freshness."

"Bah! am I a fool?" She elevated her nose.

This conversation undoubtedly explains the staidness of her demeanor that day. Not that it was necessary to keep Billy at his distance. Leaving his painful modesty out of the question, in his ignorance of the Mexican peon folk he placed her in his imagination on the same plane as a white girl, and as the color of a skin cuts no figure in the calculations of the little god, providing that it be fitted smoothly over a pretty body, she found favor in his sight. At work both the next and the following days he kept always an eye open for the flash of her white garments in the doorway. When, with the earthen jar on her head, she went to draw water from the spring his glance followed the swaying rhythms of her figure. If not actually in love by the time Don Luis and Francesca put in their appearance next morning, Billy was at least living a tropical idyl, one not a whit less beautiful because its object departed far from his ideal in all but her physical perfection.

The visit had been skilfully timed to miss lunch, and Billy was already back at his work. Crossing the bench, Don Luis's eye went instantly to the girl who had been drawn to the door by the sound of hoofbeats. But his expression gave no hint of his grim amusement. The keenest ear would have found it difficult to detect sarcasm in his remark.

"I see, señor, that you have added to your family."

Also it need not be said that Francesca's woman's eye had summed at a glance the smooth oval face, rounded arms, shapely figure; yet their undeniable comeliness brought no pleasure to her expression. If Billy had overlooked Don Luis's sarcasm it was impossible to miss her scorn.

"A capable housekeeper—if one may judge from her looks—and quite at home. You are to be congratulated, Mr. Thornton."

Looking up in quick surprise, Billy noticed the absence of the sympathy that she had shown him during her last visit. Feeling the cold anger behind, and sadly puzzled, he was not sorry when, after a few minutes of strained talk, Don Luis asked to be shown the vein. Judging by his backward glance from the mouth of the tunnel, it would appear that he had coined the request to pave the way for that which happened the instant they disappeared. For, walking her beast over to the house, Francesca spoke to the girl.

"Thy name?"

"Carmelita, señorita."

"Of what village?"

"Chilpancin—I am the daughter to Candelario, the maker of hair ropes."

Though she answered with the glib obsequiousness of her class, the appraising glance which swept Francesca from head to heel carried a mute challenge and conveyed her full knowledge that a battle was pitched such as women fight all the world over. Neither could Francesca's patrician feeling smother equal recognition. It was revealed in her next question.

"How long hast thou been in this employment?"

The girl paused. Then, whether it was due to Sebastien's tutoring or her own malice, she gave answer. "Eight days, señorita."

"Who hired thee?"

Downcast lashes hid the sudden sparkle of cunning. "Don Roberto." But they lifted in time for her to catch the sudden hardening of Francesca's face.

"Then see that thou renderest good service, for these be friends of ours."

As beforesaid, neither the cold patronage of the one nor the sullen obsequiousness of the other could hide the issue from either. Francesca's calm, as she turned her beast, did not deceive. Malicious understanding flashed out as the girl called after, "*Sí*, he shall have the best of service."

Returning to the smelter, Francesca began to talk to Caliban, yet while questioning him concerning his new employment she could not be unconscious of Carmelita lolling in the doorway, hands on shapely hips, an attitude gracefully indolent and powerfully suggestive of possession. Perhaps it was her acute consciousness of it which injected an extra chill a few minutes later into her refusal of Billy's invitation to dismount and rest. His suggestion that Seyd was likely to arrive any moment drew a still more decided shake of the head. Moreover meeting Seyd as they rode downgrade she passed with the slightest nods, nor even looked back to see if her uncle were following.

Doubtless because he felt that he could well afford it, Don Luis did stop, and before riding on he once more threatened Calixto, the rice-huller, who was with Seyd. "This fellow—he still gives good service?" His courtesy, however, did not remove the chill of Francesca's snub. Hurt and wondering, Seyd passed on up to the bench—to have his eyes opened the instant that he saw the girl in the doorway. When, after dismounting, he walked across to where Billy was at work on the foundation, her big dark eyes took him in from tip to toe in a flashing embrace. She studied him while he stood there talking.

"What is *she* doing here?"

He cut off Billy's welcome with the sharp question, and while listening to explanations his gray eyes drew into points of black. In the middle of it he burst out, "You don't mean to say that you fell for it as easily as that?"

"Fell for what?"

Billy's round eyes merely added to his irritation. "You chump! didn't you see the trap?"

"The trap?"

"Yes, trap! *T-r-a-p,* trap! Got it into your fat head? Don't you see that you have catalogued us with the San Nicolas people as a pair of blackguards forever? Oh, you fat head!"

That was not all. While he stormed on, saying things that he would willingly have taken back a minute later, every bit of its usual mercurial humor drained out of Billy's face. Over Seyd's shoulder he could see the girl in the doorway. A certain dark expectancy in her glance told that she knew herself to be the bone of contention. As a doe might watch the conflict of two bucks in the forest, she looked on, and, meeting Billy's eye, her glance touched off his anger.

"Stop that!" he suddenly yelled. "Stop it or I'll hand you one! I will, for sure! What do I care for your San Nicolas people? I didn't come down here to do a social stunt, and why should the opinions of a lot of greasers cut any ice? Let 'em go hang. The girl looks all right to me."

"All right! You innocent!" Shaking with anger, Seyd turned and spoke to Caliban, who was mixing mortar close by. "As I thought! If half he says is true her reputation would hang a cat."

But Billy's jaw only set the harder. While he might easily have been persuaded out of his idyl, he was not to be driven. Out of pure obstinacy he growled: "What of it? I reckon her morals won't spoil the food. She's proved she can cook, and that is all I want. She's going to stay."

"She's not."

"She is."

For a pause they eyed each other. Though their friendship had survived, nay, had been cemented by many a quarrel, never before had a disagreement gone such lengths.

"Look here, Billy." Seyd spoke more mildly. "This won't do. She's got to go."

"Not till you've shown me—not now," he hastily added, as Seyd began to strip. "I'd hate to hit a cripple, and—"

"Come on."

But, ducking a swing, Billy gave ground, genuine concern on his face. "No, no, old man! You are still weak. Let it go for another week. That left fin of yours—"

Landing at that precise moment on his ear, however, the member in question proved its convalescence and ended the argument by toppling him sideways. Up in a second, he closed, and for the next ten minutes they went at it, clinching and breaking, jabbing and hooking, with an energy and science that would have filled the respective souls of a moralist and a prize-fighter with disgust and delight. Avoiding both of these extreme viewpoints, the account may very well be given in the terms used by Caliban in describing the affair next day to one of his *compañeros*, a charcoal-burner.

"Like mad bulls they go at it, grappling and tearing, each striking the other so that the thud of their blows raise the echoes. It is in the very beginning that the Red Cabeza fells Don Roberto, but instead of splitting his head with the spade that stands close by—was ever such folly!—he helps him up from the ground. I then think it the finish, but no, they go at it again, hailing blows in the face hard as the kick of a mule, and so it continues for a time with only pauses to catch their breath. I am beginning to wonder will it ever come to an end when—crack! sharp as the snap of thy whip and so swift that I do not see the blow, it comes. The Red Cabeza lies there quietly on the ground. Believe it or not, Pedro, he is knocked senseless by a blow of the hand."

The immediate consequences may also be left to Caliban. "Their quarrel, as I have said, is over Carmelita, the dove of Chilpancin, and I now expect to see Don Roberto take her for his own. That she is of the same mind is proven when she comes running with her knife for him to finish up the Red Cabeza. But again, no! who shall understand these gringos?—he gives her the sharpest of looks.

"'*Vamos!* He shouts it with such anger that she stumbles and falls, running back to the house. Also she makes such a quick packing that she is driving her burro out to the trail before the Red Cabeza comes to his senses."

Billy's eyes, indeed, opened on the departing flash of her garments. "You didn't lose much time," he commented, with a quizzical glance upward. "Well, to the victor the spoils—or the rejection thereof. That was a peach of a punch—the bum left, too, wasn't it?" The old merry look flashing out again from the blood and bruises, he asked: "How'll you trade? In exchange for one admission from you I'm willing to grant you're right."

"Shoot!" Seyd grinned.

"Would you have been as careful of the proprieties if the señorita were out of the case?"

Smiling, Seyd raised doubtful shoulders. "*Quien sabe*, señor?"

"Ahem!" Billy coughed. "Now you justify the continuance of my wretched existence. All the same, while it may be correct in theory your darned morality is mighty uncomfortable practice. That girl could cook. The next time you fall in love please—"

"*Now*, what are you talking about?"

"What have I done?"

Before his look of hopeless surprise Seyd's anger faded. "I beg your pardon. Of course you didn't know, but—I'm already married."

"You?"

"Me." With grim sarcasm he added, "And you know that it is against the law of both God and man for a married man to fall in love."

Feeling dimly that something was expected of him, but debarred from congratulations by the other's irony, Billy floundered, bringing several attempts at speech to a lame conclusion. "When—when did it—happen?"

"Happen? That's it." Seyd jumped at the word. "It *happened* in New Mexico three years ago when I was down there 'experting' the Calumet group. She was the daughter of a mine foreman, pretty and neat as a grouse in the fall, but of the hopelessly common type. I don't have to describe her. You've seen them, in pairs, swinging their skirts along the boardwalks of any small town, their eyes on every man and a burst of giggles always on tap. I should never have paid her any serious attention if several of her admirers hadn't done me the honor of getting jealous. Until one big lout warned me to leave her alone under penalty of broken bones it was never more than a mild flirtation, but after that I went deeper—so deep that it was soon impossible for me to withdraw. At least, I thought it was then, though I have since come to regard my marriage with her almost as a crime. You see, I thought it would break her heart, but in less than a week after the marriage I discovered that she was nothing but a bundle of small vanities bound up in a pretty skin, that she hadn't a thought above the money and position she expected to gain through me. And how she changed! As a girl she was soft, fluffy, and innocent as a kitten, but one by one her small vanities and frivolities developed into appetites and passions, and I awoke to the fact that she was altogether animal—a beautiful animal, prettier than ever in her young wifehood, but without the slightest capacity for intellectual or spiritual development.

"If that had been all—one can love a handsome horse or a dog, and I have seen women of as low a type to be lifted out of themselves by the strength of their love. But she was absolutely selfish—loved only herself. What made it even more unbearable, she was conceited with the supreme conceit of absolute ignorance that scorns all that is unknown to itself. She would try to impose her own inch-and-a-half notions of things upon me, and she did not hesitate to pit the scraps of knowledge she had picked up around the mines against my professional training. She was bound to remold me on her own crude model. Actual wickedness would have been easier to bear, and I can assure you that the third month of our married life found me absolutely miserable. Fortunately, I received a commission just then to 'expert' a group of Mexican mines, and, as she preferred civilization as it goes in New Mexico to the hardships of a trip through the Sonora desert, I left her behind. Later I came south on a prospecting trip through the Sierra Madres, and have never seen her since."

All through he had spoken with the furious vehemence of a man easing a load off his mind. Thrusting a letter into Billy's hand, he finished, walking away: "Read that—I got it at the station yesterday. It reveals more than I could tell you in the next twenty-four hours."

And it surely did. The stiff round hand, as much as the bald statement of want and desires, revealed a nature blind to all but its own ends. Every phrase was a cry or complaint. He had no business to go off and leave her alone! All her friends agreed that it was a "shame and a disgrace." But he needn't think that she would stand such treatment forever! He had better come home, and that at once! So far she hadn't tried to "better herself." But it wasn't for lack of the chance! There was a gentleman—no fresh dude or college guy, but a rich mining man, eminently respectable, who had shown a decided interest! He (Seyd) had better look out. Thus and so did the awkward hand run over many pages, and, while Billy's eye followed, his expression gradually settled in complete disgust.

"Hopelessly common! You poor chap," he muttered, looking after Seyd, who was now helping Caliban to arrange the goods as he carried them from the mules into the adobe. "To think that you have had this on your mind all this time!" After a moment's reflection he added, "But—married or unmarried, you are still in love."

Unaware of this frank opinion, Seyd went on arranging the stores. While working, the eager vehemence of his manner settled into heavy brooding, and it was not for some time that a cheerful flash indicated his arrival at some conclusion.

"I've got it!" he murmured. And turning so suddenly that Caliban dropped the package he was carrying in, he asked, "Hast thou any acquaintance at San Nicolas?"

Reassured that the strange gringo madness was not to be vented on him, the hunchback nodded. "One of the kitchen women is daughter to my sister."

He nodded again in answer to a second question as to whether his niece could convey certain information to the señorita Francesca's ear?

"*Si*, there is always gossip moving among the women. It could be passed through Rosa, her maid."

For a man who had just taken offense at the very suggestion that he was in love Seyd's face expressed a surprising amount of satisfaction. A little sheepishly he now went on: "It must be that thou wouldst care to see thy relative? To-morrow is Sunday, and, as thy service has been good, it shall be a holiday, and thou shalt have a mule to ride to San Nicolas."

To tell the truth, the hunchback did not seem overjoyed at the prospect, at least not until Seyd tossed a silver peso on the table. "This is to buy thee meat and drink by the way, and if it be that thy niece can whisper—"

His beady eyes glittering with comprehension, the hunchback broke in, "That the dove flew at thy coming. She shall know it, señor—also from whose hand she came hither."

The quickness with which the fellow leaped to his meaning was rather disconcerting, and Seyd blushed. But, commanding his guilty colors, he brazened it out. "But see! She is not to know that it proceeds from me."

"*Si*, señor." The man's quick grin indicated an unearthly comprehension. "It will be a bit of gossip from the mouth of a muleteer."

It was at this juncture that Billy, who had just returned to work after washing the blood from his face, heard a cheerful whistling inside. When, an hour later, he went in to help with supper he found Seyd his usual cheerful self. Next morning his spirits were still higher, but did not attain their meridian until Caliban departed for San Nicolas, bravely attired in a gaudy suit which he had dug from some obscure corner of the stable. Toward evening, however, a touch of anxiety dampened his mood. It might almost have been regarded as premonitory of the news Caliban delivered in the dusk outside.

"The señorita Francesca has gone to visit her mother's people at Cuernavaca. It is not known when she will return."

"Very well; thou hast done thy share," Seyd answered.

His quiet tone, however, did not deceive the hunchback. "Did I not say these gringos were a mad people?" he demanded of Calixto, showing two pesos by the light of the stable lantern. "He pays me a peso to bring him good news, and gives me two when I return with bad—and to think that I was minded to feed him lies. Truly, there is no knowing when to have them! 'Tis the truth serves best with fools and gringos."

CHAPTER X

"

Done—at last!"

Sprawled on the flat of his back, with his curly head propped on his hands and his lime-eaten boots spread at a comfortable angle, Billy gazed upon their completed labor. The "well"—into which the liquid copper matte would presently be flowing—crucible, slag spout, blast pipes, or tuyeres, and canvas blowers, even the inclined way that led up to the platform over the loading trap, all were finished, and from the solid bed to the tip top of the brick chimney shaft Billy's vision embraced it all. Including the tons of charcoal that Caliban had burned and brought in from the woods, and the piles of ore which Seyd and Calixto had broken into smelting size with "spalling" hammers, all stood ready for the match that Seyd scratched while echoing Billy's observation.

"Done—at last!"

When the shavings and wood were fairly started under the mixed charge of charcoal and ore Seyd also lay down to watch the first smoke. Under the vigorous blast it quickly appeared—a thin blue spiral which waxed in volume and blackness. In thirty minutes it laid a sooty finger halfway across the Barranca above the hills, a sinister portent to the rancheros and peons, one that found a dark reflection in Don Luis's frown as he looked out from the upper patio of San Nicolas, far away.

Unconscious, however, of alien observation, Seyd watched the fluctuations of the black smoke with lazy enjoyment. He permitted his fancy to float with the waving pennon out over the valley down the river, where it set him aboard a log raft with his first shipment of copper matte and set him drifting down to the coast, where he could either sell to the United Metals Company or ship by sea to California smelters. There was nothing impractical about his musings. Independent of the gold values it carried, one smelting would transmute their thirty-dollar ore into copper matte worth a hundred and twenty dollars a ton. At a liberal estimate the extra twenty would pay expenses, and with a profit of a hundred dollars on an output of sixty or seventy a week during the two months before the rains, there was a small fortune in it. Next year they could both import their labor and put in a regular plant. Thereafter they would be in a position to deliver "blister" copper instead of matte to the market. Why, flaming under the breath of this first success, fancy leaped out to all sorts of possibilities, raised wharves, bunkers, storehouses in the jungle below, set a fleet of flat-bottomed sternwheelers on the river. And never was there such a river! He was traveling its long reaches in thought when fancy suddenly steered his argosy of dreams into the San Nicolas landing.

The next second he was sitting again in the shaded gallery of the upper patio, its flowers and bird song, sunshine and fountain splash in his eyes and ears. As on the other day, he watched Francesca bending over her godchild, and while he was contrasting her air of tender solicitude with the cold hauteur of her face a month ago he thought she looked up with a smile. He was answering it when the smiling eyes were wiped out by the intrusion of some unpleasant thought.

"You fool!" he chided himself. Then, sitting suddenly up, he smote Billy on the thigh with force that drew a yell of anguish. "It's a mint, boy! A blooming mint! I wouldn't trade my share for the best gold mine in Tonopah. Next year we'll put in a big plant—"

"Reverberatories with water jackets!" Billy enthusiastically took up the tale.

"Sure, and we'll build down on the flat by the river and deliver the ore by—"

"Gravity. Aerial cable—self-dumping buckets—"

"We'll refine our own matte—"

"Market our own copper and gold." His blue eyes shining, Billy ran on: "In five years we'll be rich, then for a rest and a trip. New York, London, Paris, with Nice and Monte Carlo thrown in. Europe in a touring-car, by golly! Egypt and the Pyramids! A steam yacht and a trip around the world! Hurray for us!"

"In the mean time"—Seyd led him gently back to earth—"remember, please, that this is your trick. Go and stoke up, or there'll be no Paris in yours."

And surely their days of ease lay a long way off. Long and hard as they had labored, the completion of the smelter merely marked the beginning of still more strenuous tasks. Upon them and the two peons would rest the entire weight of running the smelter at its full capacity. Besides the breaking of the ore, tapping of the slag, continuous firing, they would have to burn their own charcoal after the first supply ran out. Though they had spread the strain by dividing day and night into shifts, it would have been work enough for four times their number.

Seyd's first shift ended at twelve that night, but, though he sent Caliban off to his sleep, he himself sat up to wait for the first matte, which was due to come trickling from the spouts at any moment. Reclining his head, propped on his hand, he watched Billy and Calixto, both now of one color, each at his task, one working the blowers while the other dumped fresh ore and charcoal into the loading trap. At such times the blast would send a burst of flame high over the chimney top, lighting the house, stables, green ore mounds, showing ghostly trees beyond as under a calcium glare. Though the roar of the blast fell like a lullaby on his tired ears, excitement kept him awake till the first matte flowed in a red stream out of the tap.

"She'll go a hundred and fifty to the ton!" Billy exclaimed, after a careful examination of a cooled sample. Then, waving his hand at the huge ore mounds, he groaned: "What a shame that we hadn't enough labor and capital. We could have run it all through before the rains."

"Pig! Hog!" Seyd found a vent for his own surplus feelings by punching Billy in the chest. "Think how much worse off we should have been if we had had to mine it. Go down on your American knee bones and thank your lucky stars for the English Johnnies."

Still smiling, he lay again to watch the glowing matte as Billy ladled it out of the well. It was the culmination of their long labor, but he was too tired even to think, and, giving himself up to a dim luxurious feeling, he insensibly passed into sleep.

"Wake up, Bob, and go to bed. You still have four hours."

Only half aroused, he arose and stumbled across to the adobe, threw himself down on the bunk without waiting to remove even his boots, and fell into slumber at once so dead and dreamless that it seemed as if his head had no more than touched the pillow before Billy's voice again rang in his ear.

"Seven o'clock, Bob. I gave you an extra hour."

"Oh, quit your joshing." He murmured it, rolling over, and was again almost asleep when a sudden report, louder than thunder, but with a peculiar vibrant note, brought him swiftly to his feet. A second later the door banged to and stuck, but not before they had caught a glimpse of a huge cloud plume, densely yellow, shooting upward above the smelter.

During the moment required to wrench the door from its frame the adobe rocked under the concussion and scattered mud bricks, and there was a rain of stores from the shelves to the floor. It did not require Caliban's frightened yell on the outside, "*Explosion! Una explosion*, señores!" to tell them what had happened. The first glance, as they rushed out over the broken door, merely filled in the details of the vivid mental picture each had formed for himself. Hundreds of feet in mid air, the explosion cloud floated like a yellow balloon above the stump of a stack, the half-fused bricks of which were scattered over the bench. A cavity had been torn downward through the solid brick bed to the clay beneath, and, looking down into it, Seyd read the sign.

"Dynamite! What was the last thing you did?"

"Stoked up and sent Calixto to call Caliban while I came for you. Luckily for him that I did."

The charcoal piles were also leveled and spread over half an acre, and, walking to and fro, Seyd began to pick up and break the larger pieces. And it was only a few minutes before he called out: "Look here! Stick dynamite, broken in two and gummed over with charcoal dust—a bushel of it right here."

"Do you suppose—" Billy glanced toward the peons, who stood close by.

Seyd shook his head. "No, they had nothing to gain by it, and everything to lose. It was the easiest thing in the world for anybody to steal into the woods at night and slip a ton of this into the charcoal piles."

"Man, why didn't we think of it?" Billy groaned.

In moments of stress no two natures will express themselves in quite the same way. As they stood looking gloomily over the wreck big tears slowly forced themselves out of Billy's inflamed eyes and washed white runnels down the soot. Heartbroken, he looked up in sudden fright as Seyd burst out laughing.

"Bob! Bob!" he pleaded. "Have you gone crazy? Get a grip on yourself, there's a good fellow!"

But his pathetic anxiety merely caused Seyd to laugh the more. It was not that he was hysterical. Somehow the thought of the pain and travail, trouble, anxiety, and discomforts they had endured during the past three months touched his sense of humor.

"We have to allow that they made a pretty clean job," he said, wiping his eyes. "Let's be thankful that you were out of the way."

"Where are you going?" Billy called out, as he began to walk away.

"To finish my sleep and catch up a few hours on all that I have lost in the last three months. Take a nap yourself."

"Oh, I couldn't."

He undoubtedly thought so, yet when Seyd came out again, having slept the clock round, it was to find Billy curled up and snoring hard under the shade of the palm mat that Caliban had stretched between him and the sun. "Quit your fooling," he broke in severely on Seyd's chaffing. "Don't you know that we are down to our last dollar?"

"Thirty-three dollars and sixty cents Mex," Seyd gravely corrected. Kicking a chunk of cooled matte, he added: "But we now have this. It ought to stake us for a new start."

Billy, however, was not to be so easily separated from his grief. "Where are you going to raise capital," he demanded, "with every spare dollar in California locked up in the Nevada gold fields? If this had happened a year ago, before the Tonopah rush, we might have done it. But now?" He shook a doleful head.

"Well—New York?"

"Worse and more of it. The New Yorkers want all the bacon for killing the pig. Might as well give them the mine at once. No, Bob, it's all off. We're done—cooked a lovely brown in our own grease. Why *didn't* we guard those piles! Who do you suppose did it? Don Luis?"

Seyd shrugged. "*Quien sabe?* Doesn't look like his style. Of one thing, however, we can be certain. Your common peon doesn't habitually walk around with dynamite in his jeans. If I was going to lay any money, I'd place it on your friend Sebastien. But we haven't any time to fool on detective work. The question is—what's to be done?"

It was no light problem. As Billy had said, every dollar of Western mining capital was invested in Nevada, and Mexican projects, however good, would have to wait till the new gold fields were completely exploited. A canvass of moneyed friends yielded no results, for, while the wreck lay there under their eyes to emphasize the possibility of similar future troubles, they could not but feel it to be a hazardous venture for any person of limited means. Night brought no conclusion. But, having slept on it again, they arose and began once more, unconscious of the fact that while they lay in the heavy shade of a wild fig tree, proposing, debating, rejecting various plans, the solution was fast approaching upon its own legs.

Obviously, neither of them recognized the solution in the person of Don Luis when, about the middle of the forenoon, his horse lifted him up over the edge of the grade. On the contrary, it is doubtful whether smiling fortune was ever met with a blacker scowl than Billy's. Growling, "He's come up for a huge gloat," he would undoubtedly have returned some insult to the old man's greeting but for Seyd's stealthy kick on the shins.

Prepared as he was by the reports that charcoal-burners had brought to San Nicolas, Don Luis's face expressed his utter astonishment at the extent of the ruin. "We but heard of it last night," he told them. "It was, I suppose, accidental? I understand that these furnaces—dynamite? *Señor?*" He glanced with an interrogative frown at the peons asleep in the shade of the adobe. "It was not they?"

Reassured on that point, he nodded in confirmation of Seyd's statement that it would be foolish to hunt for the culprit. "As well try to single out a flea on a peon's dog. I warned you, señor, to expect an enemy in every stone of the Barranca. It would have been well had you listened. But"—his eyes, hands, and shoulders expressed his acceptance of fate—"it is done. And now?"

"We shall rebuild—as soon as we can raise the money."

Turning to survey the destruction, Don Luis hid a sudden gleam that was evenly compounded of admiration and irritation. When he spoke again, shrewd calculation peered from his half-closed eyes. "This time you will build a larger—"

"—Plant?" Seyd supplied the word. "No."

"But I am told, señor, that the larger the plant the greater the profits."

Seyd raised comical brows. "Fifty thousand dollars, señor—gold?"

"A small sum to your rich American capitalists."

"But we are not capitalists. No, we shall have to get along with a small furnace."

The calculation deepened in the old man's brown eyes. After a pause, to their utter astonishment, it took form in words. "But if you could raise the money?"

"What's the use of talking; we can't."

"If I were to lend it to you?"

"*You!*" It was Billy who expressed their wonder. Seyd added, after a pause, "But we have no security to offer—that is, nothing but the mine."

"And if we ran away?" Billy suggested, grinning. "Took your money and never came back?"

For the first time in their acquaintance a touch of humor lightened the heavy bronzed face. "There are some in this valley, señor, who might not count it too high a price. But as you say"—he bowed to Seyd—"the mine is security enough. Now that you have shown how, I might even work it myself. To put in a complete—"

"—Plant." Billy supplied the strange word.

"How long?"

"Between six and nine months. We should then require a little time to smelt some ore and realize. We could not—"

"*Si, si!*" In his impatience Don Luis relapsed into Spanish. "*Si*, one would not expect immediate repayment. Perhaps five thousand pesos at the end of a year—"

"Oh, we could do better than that. Ten thousand of a first payment, fifteen for the second, the remainder at a third with interest—"

"Interest? I had not thought of that." But he yielded to their insistence. "Very well, if you will have it! Shall we say five per-cent.? *Bueno!* You will, of course, have to make a trip to the United States to buy your material. If you will call at San Nicolas on your way the administrador will have letters prepared to my bankers in Ciudad, Mexico."

With a shrug that expressed relief at the conclusion he changed the subject. Riding forward to obtain a closer view of the furnace, he again clucked his surprise at the complete destruction, wagged a grave head over the half bushel of dynamite that the peons had picked out of the charcoal, curiously examined a piece of copper matte, lifting heavy brows over the statement of its values, then rode quietly away, leaving Seyd and Billy to recover as best they could from this fortunate stroke.

"Am I dreaming?" Billy's exclamation defined their mental condition. "Hit me, Bob. I want to make sure that I'm awake."

Convinced, he gasped with his first breath: "Fifty thousand dollars! By golly! Why, we can put in a complete outfit."

"Reverberatories with water jackets." Seyd took up the tale again. "We'll build down in the valley."

"Aerial cable—"

"—With iron self-dumping buckets—"

"—A flat-bottomed sternwheeler to—"

"—Take our copper down to the coast."

Blinded by the sudden light that had flashed out of their black despair they stood for some time looking out over the Barranca with shining eyes which saw a small mining town rising out of the jungle's tangles. It was fully ten minutes before Seyd came back to earth.

"I wonder what is behind all this? Seems rather funny that the old chap should come to our help?"

"Not knowing, can't say and don't care a darn! So far as I am concerned, at fifty thousand a throw he can be just as inconsistent as he jolly well likes."

"Nevertheless," Seyd mused, "I'd give three cents to know."

Meanwhile, Don Luis pursued his quiet way, now at a heavy canter, again on a stately trot, through the jungle out to the first village beyond the forks of the trail. As he passed the little *fonda* Sebastien Rocha rode out from a group of rancheros who stood drinking at the rough bar.

"They told me of the passing," he said, nodding backward. "And I waited. What news? Did the gringos go up with their furnace? No? Still they will now have their bellies full of Guerrero?"

But his face dropped at Don Luis's answer. "No, they are to build again."

"But I thought—was it not the agent at the station who said they had no money?"

"Neither had they." It was always difficult to read the massive face, but now it expressed just a shade of malicious amusement. "I have lent them fifty thousand pesos."

"*Thou!*" For once the man's usual cynical calm was completely disrupted. In his vast astonishment he whispered it: "*Thou? Fifty thousand pesos?*"

"*Yo.*" Smiling slightly, he went on: "Now listen, Sebastien. Not to mention thy little attempt on their virtue, this is the third on their lives, and all badly bungled. So do not wonder that I thought it time to take them into my own hand. Now that they are there, let there be no mistake—the meddling finger is likely to be badly pinched. From this time—they are *mine*."

"But—why give them money?"

"To forestall others." Had he been there to hear, the following words would fully have answered Seyd's question. "The elder of these lads is no common man. By hook or by crook he would have raised a company—if he had to rope and tie down his men on the run. Then, instead of these two, we should have a dozen gringos, with Porfirio and his rurales to back up their charter. But do not fear."

From the cleared fields through which they were riding it was possible to see Santa Gertrudis, and, turning in his saddle, he extended his quirt toward its green scar.

"Do not fear."

CHAPTER XI

It was in the middle of the rainy season. Stepping out of his office, where he had just added a few drops of Scotch to the water he was absorbing at every pore, the station agent came face to face with the engineer of the down train.

"Nine hours late?" The engineer gruffly repeated the other's comment. "We are lucky to be here at all. Besides being sopping wet, the wood we're burning is that dosey it'd make a fireproof curtain for hell. This kind of railroading don't suit my book, and I'm telling you that if they don't serve us out something pretty soon that smells like wood I know one fat engineer that will be missing on this line." Jerking his thumb at the lone passenger who had descended at the station, he added: "But for that chap we'd never have got through. When the track went out from under us at La Puente he pitched in and showed us no end of wrinkles. If you've got anything inside just give him a nip for me."

"Hullo, Mr. Seyd!" Coming face to face with the passenger after the train had gone on, the agent thrust out his hand. "What a pity you weren't on the other train. She was twenty hours late—in fact, only pulled out a couple of hours ago. Miss Francesca was aboard, and she just left."

"Not alone?"

The agent laughed. "Sure! She don't care. Three weeks ago she came galloping in through one of the heaviest rains and took the up train."

"So she has been home since I left?"

"Let me see—that's nigh on three months, isn't it? Sure, she came home just after you left."

With this bit of information lingering in the forefront of his mind Seyd, a little later, rode out from the station. Not that it engrossed, by any means, the whole of his thought. Even had he been free, the hard work and bitter disappointment of the first venture, and the equally hard thought and careful planning for the second during his long absence in the States, would have been sufficient to keep her in the background. If he had never happened to see Francesca again she would probably have lingered as an unusually pretty face in the gallery of his mind. While it was only natural that he should wonder if the news that he sent in by Caliban had ever reached her ear, it was merely a passing thought. His mind soon turned again to his plans. Up to the moment that, four hours later, he came slipping and sliding downhill upon her she was altogether out of his thought.

For that very reason his fresh senses leaped to take the picture she made standing in the gray sheeting rain beside her fallen horse, and through its very difference from either the tan riding habit or virginal batiste of his memory her loose waterproof with its capote hood helped to stamp this figure upon his brain. Before she said a word he had gone back to the feelings of four months ago.

The pelting rain had washed all but a few clay streaks off her coat. Touching them, she explained: "The poor beast fell under me. I fear it has broken a leg."

While speaking she offered her hand; and if that had not been sufficient, her friendly smile more than answered his speculation. Caliban's niece had certainly done her duty! Indeed, while he was stooping over the fallen animal a quick glance upward would have given him a look evenly compounded of mischief and remorse. It gave place to sudden sorrow when he spoke.

"It is broken, all right. There is only one thing to be done. If you will lead my horse around the shoulder of the hill I will put the poor thing out of its pain."

Her life had been cast too much in the open for her to be ignorant of the needs of the case. Nevertheless, he saw that her eyes were brimming as she led his horse away; and, remembering their black fire on the day that she had ordered the charcoal-burners flogged, he wondered. It would have been even harder to reconcile the two impressions had he seen the tears rolling down her cheeks when the muffled report of his pistol followed her around the hill. But she had wiped them away before he rejoined her. If the sensitive red mouth trembled, her voice was under control.

"No, I had not waited long," she answered his question. "You see, the poor creature lost a shoe earlier in the day, and I had to ride back to have it replaced. It would have been better had I stayed there."

For the moment he was puzzled. An hour ago he had ridden past the last habitation, a flimsy hut already overcrowded with the peon, his wife, their children, chickens, and pigs. All around them stretched wide wastes of volcanic rock and scrub. They were, as he knew, on the hacienda San Angel, but the buildings lay five leagues to the north. With hard riding he had expected to make the inn at the foot of the Barranca wall that night. She might do it by taking his horse. But if anything went wrong? She would be alone—all night—in the rain! He felt easier when she refused the offer of his beast.

"And leave you to walk? No, sir."

A second offer to walk by her side not only ran counter to the prejudice of a race of riders, but also aroused her sympathies. "I could never think of it!"

After a moment of thought she propounded her own solution. "Your beast is strong. I have ridden double on an animal half his size. We will both ride."

Now, though Seyd had long ago grown to the sight of rancheros on their way to market in the embrace of their buxom brown wives, the suddenness of it made him gasp. But by a quick mounting he succeeded in hiding the rush of blood to his face. Also he managed to control his voice.

"Fine idea! Give me your hand."

Just touching his foot, she rose like a bird to the croup. When, as the horse moved on, she slid an arm around his waist his demoralization was full and complete. If he glanced down it was to see her fingers resting like small white butterflies on his raincoat. Did he look up, then a faint perfume of damp hair would come floating over his shoulder. He thrilled when her clasp tightened as the horse broke into a gentle trot, and was altogether in a bad way when her merry laugh restored order among his senses.

"Now we can play Rosa and Rosario on their way to market. It will be for you to grumble at prices while I rail at the government tax that puts woolens beyond the purse of a peon."

"I prefer to ask what brought you out in such weather." He returned her laugh. "A pretty pickle you would have been in if I had not come along."

He felt the vigorous shake of her head. "I should have walked back to the last hut, and an oxcart would have taken me in to the station."

"But then you would have been out all night."

"I should have loved it." Though he did not see the sudden blooming under her hood, he felt the unconscious squeeze which testified to the sincerity of her feeling. "I love them—the roar of the wind, black darkness, the beat of the rain in my face. Mother would have had me stay in Mexico till the rains were over, but when Don Luis wrote that the river was at flood nothing could hold me." He had thrilled under her unconscious pressure, but her conclusion proved an excellent corrective. "I am afraid that the site for your new buildings must be under water."

"How can that be?" He spoke quickly. "We are building well back from last year's mark, and Don Luis said that it was the highest known."

"But this year it has gone even higher—and all because of the Yankee companies that are stripping the upper valley of timber. There were great fires, too, last year which broke away from their servants and burned hundreds of miles of woods."

Her quiet answer went far to allay his sudden suspicion, but not his anxiety. He spoke of Billy. "It is over a month since he came out to the station for stores, and the agent told me that none of your people had seen him for weeks."

"But he has with him Angelo"—she gave Caliban his correct name—"and he, as I once told you, was counted Sebastien's best man in his war against the brigands. Though he may not show it to you, he is not ungrateful for the gift of his life. If food is to be had in the country, Mr. Thornton will not go lacking."

He spoke more cheerfully. "Then I don't care; though if the site *is* flooded we shall be thrown back at least three months with our work."

"And what is three months?" she added, laughing.

To him it was a great deal. Before paying over the loan Don Luis's lawyers had taken Seyd's signatures upon certain instruments which exhibited the General in the new light of a shrewd and conservative business man. Withal, having still plenty of time, he answered quite cheerfully when she turned the conversation with a question concerning his plans. Under the stimulation of her curiosity, which surprised him by its intelligence, he went into details, talking and answering her questions while the horse trudged steadily on into the darkening rain. If the trail had not suddenly faded out, night would have caught them unnoticed.

In that volcanic country, where for long stretches a hoof left no impression, the loss of a trail was a common experience, and, trusting to the instinct of the beast, Seyd gave it the rein. Left to its own devices, however, it gradually swerved from the beating rain and presently turned on to a cattle track which swung away into gum copal trees and scrub oak at an imperceptible angle. Had he been alone Seyd would have soon noticed the absence of the Aztec ruin. As it was, but not until an hour later, Francesca was the first to speak.

"That's so," he agreed, when she drew his attention. "We ought to have passed it long ago. The animal evidently picked up a wrong track coming out from the rocks." After a moment's reflection he said: "It would be worse than foolish to try to go back. We could never find the trail in this black rain. Better follow on and see where it will bring us." With a sudden remembrance of what it might mean to her, a young girl brought up in the rigid conventions of the country, he repentantly added: "I'm awfully sorry for you. I ought to be kicked for my carelessness."

"No, I have traveled this trail much oftener than you," she quietly protested. "If any one is blamed I should be the one."

Sitting there in black darkness, lost in those lonely volcanic hills, with the rain dashing in his face and the roar of the wind in his ears, he was prepared to appreciate her quiet answer. "You are a brick!" he exclaimed. "Nevertheless, I feel my guilt."

"Then you need not." She gave a little laugh. "Did I not say that I enjoyed being out at night in the rain?"

"And now the gods have called your bluff."

"*Bluff?*" She laughed again at the meaning of that rank Americanism. "It was no bluff, as you will presently see."

And see he did—during the long hour they spent splashing along in black darkness, up hill, down dale, fording swollen arroyos, through chaparral which tore at them with myriad claws and wet woods whose boughs lashed their faces. Up to the moment that the roof of a hut suddenly loomed out against the dim, dark sky she uttered no doubt or complaint. When, having tied his horse under the wide eaves, he lit a match inside, its flare revealed her face, quiet and serene.

Also it showed that which, while not nearly so interesting, had its immediate uses—a candle stuck in a *tequila* bottle; and its steadier flare presently helped them to another find—a chemisette and other garments of feminine wear, spotlessly clean and smoothly ironed, arranged on a string that ran over a bunk in one corner.

"The fiesta wear of our hostess," Francesca remarked. "How lucky! for I am drenched."

"And look at that pile of dry wood!" he exclaimed. "The gods are with us. I'll build a fire, then while I rub down the horse you can change. What's this?"

It was a rough sketch done with charcoal on the table. Two parallelograms with sticks for legs were in furious pursuit of certain horned squares which, in their turn, were in full flight toward a doll's house in the far corner.

"Oh, I know!" the girl cried, after a moment of study. "Here, in the wild country where they never see man, are raised the fighting bulls for the rings of Mexico. This hut belongs to a vaquero of San Angel, and this is an order, left in his absence, to drive the bulls into the hacienda." Laying her finger on a triangle which had evidently been added later, she continued, laughing: "This shows that his woman has gone with him. They were evidently called away unexpectedly, for she had already set the corn to soak in this *olla* for the supper tortillas. And the saints be praised! Here are dried beef, salt, and chilis. Now hurry the fire, and you shall see what a cook I am."

While he was building it in the center of the mud floor she made other finds—a cube of brown sugar, coffee, a cake of goat's cheese; and her little delighted exclamations over each discovery both amused him and proved how sincere was her acceptance of the situation. "She's a brick!" he told the horse, rubbing him down, outside, with wisps pulled out from the under side of the thatch. "Thoroughbred in blood and bone." As the animal had already experimented with the thatch and found it quite to its liking, the question of provender was settled. But in order that Francesca might have ample time to change, Seyd rubbed and rubbed and rubbed till a rattle of clay pots inside gave him leave to come in.

At the door he paused to admire the picture she made in the red glow of the fire. In place of the slender girl of the stylish raincoat a pretty peona raised velvet eyes from the stone *metate* on which she was vigorously rubbing soaked corn for the supper tortillas. By emphasizing some features and softening others strange attire always gives a new view of a woman. The sleeveless garment showed the round white arms and foreshortened and filled out her slender lines.

Glancing down at her arms, she confessed, with an uneasy wriggle: "I don't like it, though I wear décolleté every evening when we are in the city. But I shall soon get used to it."

Conscious of his admiring eyes, she found them employment in watching the tortillas. But, having grown accustomed to the new dress by the time supper was ready, she left him free to watch the white arms and small hands which hovered like butterflies over the clay pot. In the lack of all other utensils, they used bits of tortilla for spoons, dipping alternately into the pot which she had set between them; nor did he find the chili any the worse for its contact with the tortilla which had just taken an impression of her small teeth. It required only an after-dinner pipe, to which she graciously consented, to seal his content.

After the wet and fatigue of the trail the warmth and cheer of food and fire were extremely grateful, but not conducive to talk. While he sat watching the tobacco smoke curl up into the blackened peak of the roof she leaned, chin in her hands, elbows on crossed knees, studying the fire. Leaping out of red coal, an occasional flame set its reflection in her deep eyes, and as his gaze wandered from her around the rough *jacal* Seyd found it difficult to realize that it was indeed he, Robert Seyd, mining engineer of San Francisco, who sat there sharing food and fire with a girl, on the one hand scion of the Mexican aristocracy, descendant on the other of a line which ran back into the dim time of the Aztecs. The thought stirred the romance within him and helped to prolong his silence. It would have held him still longer if his musings had not been suddenly interrupted by her merry laugh.

"Si?" he inquired, looking suddenly up.

"I was thinking what they would say—my mother, Don Luis, the neighbors?"

"Horrible!" he agreed. "Your mother? What would she say?"

As the white hands flew up in a horrified gesture it was the señora herself. *"Santa Maria Marissima!"*

"And Don Luis?"

Her expression changed from laughter into sudden mischievous demureness. "His remarks, señor, are not for me to repeat."

"Well—the neighbors?"

Once more her hands went up. "'Was it not that we always said it of that mad girl! Maria, thou shalt not speak with her again.'" Smiling, she added, "For you must know, señor, that I have been held as a horrible example of the things a girl should not do since the days of my childhood."

"Like the devil in the old New England theology," he suggested, smiling, "you make more converts than the preacher?"

He had to explain before she understood. Then she laughed merrily. "Just so. What they would do were I to marry, die, or reform, I really cannot tell. It would leave a gap almost equal to the loss of the catechism." She finished with a mock sigh, "They will never appreciate me till I'm dead."

"Any present danger?"

The smiling mouth pursed demurely under his whimsical glance. "I am afraid not. You saw my performance at supper. I am the despair of my mother, who would have me more delicate and refined."

"Marriage?"

"No one wants me."

"Don Sebastien?"

It slipped out, and he was immediately sorry, but she only laughed. "Tut! tut! A cousin?"

Surveying him from under drooping lashes, a glance soft and warm as velvet, she added: "I will confess. There *were* others. Some too fat, some too thin, all too stupid, here at home. In Mexico they were triflers—or worse. But on the honor of a lone maid, señor, never a man among them." With a sudden relapse into seriousness she repeated, "Among *all* of them—never a man." Though she was looking directly at him, her glance seemed to go on, fly to some further vision which, for one second, set its reflection in her eyes. Then her long silky lashes wiped it out. When they rose again it was over mischievous lights. "Never a *man*," with a change of accent.

"But he will come—some day," he teased.

"And go—after the fashion of dream men."

"And dream women."

For a while she studied him curiously. "Then she has not come?"

"Yes," he answered, with sudden impulse. "But—"

She softly filled the pause. "'But' and 'because' are woman's reasons."

"Unhappily, sometimes man's," he gravely answered; and, feeling, perhaps, that the conversation was drifting into unsafe latitudes, he rose and began to pull dry grass from the under side of the thatch. "For you," he exclaimed, with a glance at the bunk. "I knew you wouldn't care to sleep there."

Having arranged a thick layer at a safe distance from the fire, he gathered another armful, and was going outside when she called him back. "To make my bed," he answered her question.

"In the wet?"

"Oh, it isn't so bad—here under the eaves."

"Only an inch of water," she answered him, with pretty sarcasm; and, indicating certain small trickles that were coming through the cane siding, she gave him his orders. "You will sleep here—inside."

"But—" he began.

"Señor, I said that you would sleep *inside*."

As a matter of fact, the "prospect" outside was not inviting, and his acquiescence lowered the quick colors his previous obstinacy had raised. She had already settled down on one elbow; and when, having arranged a bed on the opposite side of the fire, he lit a second pipe, she studied him through the smoke, wondering what pictures were responsible for his earnest gaze. But warmth and comfort presently produced their natural effect, and she began to nod. After a few shy, sleepy glances that showed him still staring moodily into the fire her head sank upon the white fullness of her doubled arm.

As a matter of fact, it was his wife's face that returned his steady gaze from a nest of red coal. Absorbed in bitter musings, he received the first intimation of Francesca's sleep from a sigh which caused him to start as though at the report of a gun. Then while the warm blood streamed through his drumming pulses, every sense vividly alive, he looked down upon her. With all the timid awe that Adam must have displayed when he awoke to the sight of Eve he studied this greatest of masculine experiences, a woman clad in the soft armor of sleep.

For some time his senses dwelt only on the fact, and gave him merely the soft sigh of her sleep, the play of firelight over the unconscious figure. But presently his mind began to work, to compare the broad forehead, oval contours, fine-cut nostrils, delicate chiseling of her features, with the common prettiness of his wife. Even the little foot and slender ankle, freed by relaxation from the jealous skirt, helped to emphasize differences wide as those between a hummingbird and a pouter pigeon. It had required the rigid selection of a thousand generations, the pre-eminence in strength and brains of a line of fighters to produce the one, just as the slacker choice of a commoner breed had created the other; and Seyd, whose own blood had come down through the clean channels of good Colonial stock, recognized the fact. As never before he was impressed with the fatuity of his chivalric rashness. While the firelight rose and fell he strained at the ties which stretched over mountains, desert, plains, binding him to the coarse woman in Albuquerque.

His sudden jerk forward was the physical equivalent of his mental strain. Though homely, even slangy, his mutter, "Your cake is baked, son. The sooner you let this girl know it the better," was none the less tragic. The thought was the last in his waking mind.

Before going to sleep he performed one last service. Noticing that she shivered under the wet breath of the night, he took off his coat, tiptoed across, and, after laying it softly across her shoulders, returned with equal caution. She did not stir or even change the slow rhythm of her breath, but he had no more than lain down before her eyes slowly opened. When his deep respirations told that he was fast asleep she rose on one elbow and looked at him across the fire.

In her turn, with glances shyly curious as those with which Eve, newly formed, may have eyed Adam still in "deep sleep," she noted the wide-spaced, deep-set eyes, strong nose, the ideality of the brows, the humorous puckers at the corners of his mouth. Though she did not analyze their individual meanings, the totality made a strong appeal to instinct and intuitions formed by the vast experience of the race. Her impression phrased itself in her murmur, "A wholesome face."

Only the cleft chin seemed to carry a special meaning. Surveying it, a gleam of mischief shot through the soft satisfaction of her look, and she murmured beneath her breath in Spanish, "Oh, fickle! fickle! Thy wife will need the sharpest of eyes."

The thought brought a little laugh, and for a minute thereafter she sat, a finger upon her lip, listening for a break in his breathing. When it did not come she rose slowly, stole like a mouse across the floor, and laid his coat, light as a feather, over his unprotected shoulders. Back again on her own couch, she looked across at him again; a glance naïve in its enjoyment of the romantic impropriety of the entire proceeding. Then, curling up under her raincoat, she fell fast asleep.

CHAPTER XII

Thoroughly fagged out by six weary nights on the train, Seyd slept like the dead, and did not awaken until a sudden clatter of pots aroused him to knowledge of a golden cobweb of light streaming in between the flimsy siding of the hut. Through the open doorway he obtained a glimpse of a bejeweled world, resonant with the song of birds. After informing him of these facts, his eyes reintroduced him to the young lady in the tan riding habit who had ousted the pretty peona of last night from her command over fire and dishes. The satisfying odor of hot coffee completed the verdict of his senses.

"Breakfast all ready? I must have slept like a log."

"You did." She laughed. "I rattled the dishes in vain. I was just about to throw something at you."

Now, his last waking thought had outlined a purpose to inform her at once of his marriage, and while they were eating breakfast it recurred again. But not with the same force. That which, when imbued with the sentimental values of firelight and silence, appeared necessary and right somehow appeared almost absurd when viewed in broad day. Checking sentiment, too, by its very friendliness, her manner did not invite confession.

"It would be impertinent," he concluded. "She has no personal interest in me."

If he had observed her only an hour earlier re-entering the *jacal* after a shivering exchange outside with the peona he might not have been quite so sure. Once or twice she had indulged in softer thought, whose key was to be found in her murmur just before she tried to awake him:

"*Adios*, Rosario."

Also the morning had brought its own problem to fill his mind. He could not but see that their appearance at the inn in the Barranca so early in the day would be a confession of their breach of the most rigid of Spanish conventions. But how to broach the subject without offense? Though he racked his brains while saddling the horse and, later, when it was carrying them double upon their way, he had come to no conclusion up to the moment that she settled it herself with a little cry.

"Now I know where I am." She was indicating an outcropping of rock on a sterile hillside. "We strayed miles away from our trail. We shall soon come to a path that leads past a rancho where I can borrow a horse."

Almost as they spoke the cattle track they had been following joined a trail, and shortly after she spoke again, laughing. "And now, Señor Rosario, I must bid you good-by. This good beast has done nobly, but we shall gain time if one rides forward to the rancho and sends back a horse. Which shall it be?"

But he was already on the ground, hat in hand. "Rosa, *adios*."

Laughing, she rode on while he sat down on an outcropping of rock to wait, for he was not minded to wade through the wet grass and brush of some woods at the foot of the hill. Until she passed from sight he sat watching, then, feeling a little lazy, he fitted his angles into a sort of natural couch in the rock and fell to musing, reviewing again the incidents of the night. He had not intended to sleep. But what with the warmth and stillness, he presently passed quietly away, was still unconscious when the stroke of a hoof on a rock awoke him to the sight of two horsemen with a led beast.

"For me," he thought. Then, as he recognized Sebastien Rocha in the second horseman, he whistled his consternation. If the hacendado had not actually met Francesca he must surely have pumped the *mozo* dry, and now the sight of him, Seyd, would fully reveal their case!

"Now for a big fat row," he told himself. But, greatly to his surprise, Sebastien passed on with a nod, and presently turned from the trail, following their fresh hoof tracks over the hill. The *mozo* had already gone on to retrieve Francesca's saddle from the dead horse, and, irritated and alarmed, Seyd mounted the led beast and rode on at a gallop. But, quickly realizing that his further company was not likely to improve the girl's case, he presently pulled the beast back to a walk. Lost in frowning thought, he rode on slowly until, an hour later, there came a beat of galloping hoofs, and Sebastien rode up from behind.

His reiteration of the thought "Now for the row!" was colored by the way in which the hacendado's hand went to his holster. But Seyd's hand, which moved as quickly to his own gun, dropped, and he blushed crimson as the other held out his brier pipe.

"Merely *this*, señor." He glanced meaningly at Seyd's gun. "For *that* you would have been too late. I could have shot you through the back. After this do not let your foolish Yankee pride stop you from looking behind."

Though both angry and alarmed, the cold impudence of it made Seyd laugh. "Yes? How did you resist the temptation?"

"It was a temptation." He gravely approved the word. "Your back made such a fine smooth mark. I could see the bullet splash in the center."

"Then why didn't you? Since you are so frank I don't mind saying that I believe that you already had a hand in at least one of three attempts on my life! Is it that you would prefer to have me blown up?"

"Like your predecessor, the Hollander?" Sebastien's shrug might have meant anything. "I have, of course, my preferences, and some day I shall have to decide in just which way I would wish you put to death. In passing the opportunity now you ought to feel complimented, for let me tell you that I would never leave any Mexican lips free to tell of your experiences last night."

The man's tone of quiet certainty robbed the words of extravagance; and, accustomed now to a life that out-melodramaed melodrama, Seyd knew better than to take them for jest. "That's very nice of you," he quietly answered, and as just then the trail narrowed to pass through a copal grove he added: "Forewarned is forearmed. Just to keep you out of temptation— will you please to go first?"

"With pleasure."

Faint though it was, the smile that loosened the firm mouth made it easier for Seyd to continue when they were riding once more side by side. "For the young lady's sake I am glad to have you take such a sensible view of an unavoidable situation. I take it that you were going the other way. If you can trust me—"

"Trust no one and you will never be deceived. If I had my way of it there would be an end to the girl's wild tricks. But since she *will* be abroad, what better escort could she have than her kinsman?"

"None," Seyd agreed. "I overtook her by accident, cared for her the best that I could; now she is in your hands."

Sebastien shook his head. "Not so swiftly. She would hardly thank me for your dismissal." While the shadow of a smile lifted the corner of his thin lips he added: "The last time I mixed in her affairs she refused to speak with me for over a year, and I have no mind to repeat the experience. We are all going to San Nicolas. It would be foolish to ride apart."

"Very well," Seyd agreed, not, however, with any great degree of pleasure. Apart from the strain involved by a day's travel with a man who had just confessed to a permanent intention of killing him he felt more disappointment than he would have cared to admit at the spoiling of the tête-à-tête with the girl. In fact, the feeling was so acute that he found it necessary to justify it in his own thought. "It was only for a day," he mused, slightly changing his previous conclusion to fit the case, "and I'd like to have seen it out."

"So! so! The storm proved a little too much for this one."

They had just ridden into copal woods, and, looking up, Seyd saw that he was pointing at a pile of bones and wet tatters of clothing that lay under a swinging fray of rope. If possible, it was more grisly of appearance than a second mummy which still swung, clicking its miserable bones in the wind. Whether or no he noticed Seyd's shiver of disgust Sebastien ran easily on:

"He was a stout rogue, this fellow, with a keen eye for a pretty woman and small scruples as to how he got her. It was, indeed, through this little weakness that we caught him, using a girl to bait the trap. But he died game—with a joke on his lips. 'Señor,' he said, as the mule went from under him, 'if but one-half of my brats walk in my steps thou wilt have need of an army to finish us up.'

"He had humor, too. He it was that stole the altar service from the church of San Anselmo to pay the priest of Guadaloupe to say a thousand masses for the repose of his soul. He was dead and the masses said before the service was traced by a pilgrim to the Guadaloupe shrine, and ever since the priests have been at war—both over the return of the service and to decide the burning question as to whether it is possible to nullify a heavenly title obtained through fraud. It makes a pretty point in theology, and the battle still rages. Being debarred from physical expression, the brute in a priest exercises itself through the tongue, and they will not leave such a choice morsel till the last shred of meat has been gnawed from the bones."

In presence of those dumb witnesses to its truth, the grim banter sounded even grimmer. During the long white nights that followed hard days at work on the smelter nothing had suited Caliban more than to be drawn on to talk of the war against the brigands. Under the red light of a camp fire, with the vast night of the Barranca yawning below, the tales had been spun—tales that had outdone the dime novels of Seyd's youth. Of them all, that which had ended with the hanging of the last bandit in this very glade had outdone all in sheer desperation.

Kindling to the romance of it all, he took stealthy note, as they rode on, of the lithe muscular figure, which was as extraordinary in its balanced strength as the calm power of the quiet brown face. When memory drew a vivid contrast between Sebastien and his early training in the sober atmosphere of the English commercial boarding-school Seyd wondered, and finally put his wonder into words.

"Didn't you find the transition from Manchester rather sudden? It must have been like plunging head first into a romance."

"Romance?" For the first time that morning, for matter of that, in all their intercourse, Sebastien laughed outright. "Oh, you Anglo-Saxons! Romance is a creature of your own dreamy idealism. We do not know it. We are passionate, nervous, hysterical, gross, materialistic, but for all our heat we see life more clearly than you. It would be better for us if we did not. For where in the mirror of your imaginings you see your strength enormously magnified our clearer perceptions show our weaknesses. Even at the point of death you neither see nor accept defeat. But we, cowering before it, are swept the quicker away." Just as on that other occasion when he stood talking beside their fire on the rim of the Barranca, this came out of his quiet with volcanic heat. Dropping as quickly into his usual calm, he finished, "No, I did not find it romantic—merely amusing."

Nettled a little by his amused contempt, Seyd quickly retorted: "I fail to see how you can claim to have no ideals? You who are striving with all your might against the American invasion?"

Sebastien shrugged. "Racial aversion—backed up by the instinct of self-preservation. Even cattle will band together against the wolves. But remove the danger and the bulls fall at once fighting for command of the herd. Before Diaz we had sixty-five rulers in sixty years, very few of whom died in their beds. Once remove his iron hand from our throats and we shall go at it again, revolution upon revolution, for the sole purpose of satisfying some man's personal ambition, lust, or individual greed. No, señor, we are individualists in the extreme. We have nothing in our make-up to correspond to the racial ideal that makes you Northmen subordinate personal interest to the general good. And because of our lack you will eventually rule us."

"Yet you strive against it?"

"For the one reason, as I told you, that the weaker wolf declines to be eaten. Individually, I find it amusing. I would much prefer shooting gringo soldiery to hanging Mexican bandits."

"And the General—Don Luis?"

Once again Sebastien laughed. "That old revolutionist? He would deny all I have said as rank heresy, though he himself is its most startling example. He would say that he was for Mexico, but Mexico, to him, is Mexico with a Garcia for president. Selfish to the backbone, every one of us."

In a phrase he had described Don Luis, and, while he could not but smile at its truth, Seyd was just a little startled by the keen intelligence and flashing intuition. Even after allowing for advantages of travel and education the man's sharp reasoning and originality were remarkable. Like a clear black pool his mind sharply reflected all that passed over it, and always the conception stood out as under a lightning flash.

"No, señor," he went on, after a pause, "we are individualists, and as such can only obtain happiness by following our own bent. If we are held back for a while by Porfirio, be sure that sooner or later we shall return with greater zest to our ancient pastime of cutting each other's throats."

His uncanny intelligence, too, threw sinister lights on everything they passed. "I told you we were gross," he said, indicating a youth and a brown girl who were flirting through the barred windows of an adobe ranch house. "The proof—the bars. With us love is a passion; the ideal exists only in our songs."

Shortly thereafter they rode out on the rim overlooking the Barranca, and the necessity of riding in single file down the zigzag staircases brought an end to their talk. Neither did he begin it again as they crossed the bottom flat to the inn. Coming after a long silence, the invitation which he delivered at last, as they rode into the patio, came as a greater surprise.

"I feel certain, señor, that my cousin will wish you to lunch with us."

Because another trait in Sebastien's nature was not revealed until, a few minutes later, he knocked at Francesca's door, Seyd failed to see that which, after all, was perhaps even more surprising. As he entered in response to her call she rose and stood, one hand resting on the small altar where burned a tiny taper; and as he stood looking at her across the length of the room the inquiry in her wide eyes became touched with fear.

"It is you?" she broke the silence. "They told me that you spent last night here. How was it that I did not meet you on the way?"

"Simply because I had happened to turn in at the Rancho del Rio to look at some cattle. But I overtook the *mozo* you sent back with the horse for the gringo. Also I called in at the *jacal* of Miguel, the vaquero of San Angel, where I found Maria, his woman, just returned. She was rejoicing over a supernatural visitation. It seems that while she and Miguel were away the Virgin Guadaloupe abode in their house, and even honored Maria by putting on her best fiesta clothes. In proof thereof she showed me a silver peso that the Virgin left tied up in one corner of her chemisette. It was truly remarkable, and I was well on my way to a healthy conversion when I happened to stumble on the gringo's pipe—at least, he claimed it on sight."

"And you immediately turned about to tattle this to me?"

He merely smiled under her bright scorn. "To see you home."

"Where you will proceed to make my mother eternally miserable, and uncle—"

"—Infernally angry? On the contrary, I am prepared to back up with pistol and knife the tale of Maria's visitation. Why should I wish to bring suffering to the good mother? It was a hap of the trail, and, much as I hate all gringos, it was far better that you should have been in this man's hands. Some day I may have to kill him, and I shall do it with greater pleasure because of this!"

"If the attempt does not fail as miserably as that which you made on his soul."

"Put it morals, cousin, just to bring it within the bounds of my comprehension. You know my beliefs as to souls."

"In any case it was a mean trick."

"Tricks are tricks only when they fail. Successful, they rise to the dignity of strategems. And he ought not to complain. Did he not come out of the ordeal unscathed, tricked out in the flowers of virtue? He's really in my debt. But returning to my point, some day I shall kill him; but in the mean time I have asked him to lunch with us. As he looked hungry, I should suggest a little haste."

"I am ready now." Going toward him, she spoke, hesitantly: "Let me—thank you. Were you always thus, Sebastien, we should be better friends."

"*Gracias*, anything but that." Bowing, he stood aside to permit her to pass. "The half liking that you deal out to Anton, Javier, and other fat-jowled hacendados, your admirers, would never do for me. I prefer your—fear."

"But I am not afraid of you." She looked straight in his eyes passing out.

"You will be—some day."

CHAPTER XIII

Coming out from luncheon—at which Sebastien had presided with a grave courtesy which lifted the inn's humble fare of eggs, tortillas, and rice to epicurean heights—Seyd and Francesca came face to face with Tomas, her *mozo*, who had just ridden into the patio. At sight of his mistress the *mozo's* teeth flashed in the golden dusk under his sombrero, but he shook his head when she reached for the letter which he took out of his saddle bags.

"It is for the gringo señor. The *jefe* did not know of your coming."

It was, of course, from Don Luis. Couched in terms massively dignified as his own reserve, it apologized for the floods as for some personal fault, and finished by placing hacienda San Nicolas at Seyd's service.

"So you will ride on with us," Francesca commented upon its content.

As Sebastien had gone to order fresh horses, there was no one but Seyd to observe her evident pleasure. But if he thrilled, yet he persisted, pleading that he intended to establish headquarters there at the inn and would be head over heels in business, freighting machinery and supplies in from the station.

He smiled at her further objection that he would hardly find the accommodations of the inn to his liking. "They are better than at the mine. If they prove too bad I shall run down to San Nicolas to beg a meal."

"Very well, señor, we shall expect you."

Her little backward nod, riding away with Sebastien a few minutes later, reaffirmed it, but while Seyd bowed in acknowledgment his thought ran oppositely. Unaware how quickly circumstances would compel the visit, he formulated a hardy resolution. "Now, young man, no more sentimental fooling. It's you for work. The first thing is to get across to Billy."

When, however, he took counsel with his fat brown host concerning the hire of a dugout the latter held up pudgy hands in horror. *Santissimo Trinidad!* The very idea was madness! With the river running a mile wide at its narrowest? Not a peon would venture upon it! And under the inspiration of his belief that a live customer was to be preferred to even a drowned gringo he worked privately against Seyd's suicidal intention. So well did he scatter his pessimistic seed that when Seyd succeeded in finding a dugout he had to buy it outright; nor could he persuade a single peon to dare the flood.

It was while returning to the inn late in the day that he obtained his first glimpse of the river from a knoll which lifted him above the drowned jungle. Around wooded islands, which were usually dry hills, a waste of waters, thick and brown as chocolate, swept madly. Along the edge of the jungle it boiled in fat eddies which sucked and licked the trailing greenery. Farther out it was whipped into a yellow cream by the thrashing branches of uprooted trees, ceibas and cedars, huge as a church, which rolled and tumbled as their submerged limbs caught on the bottom. Everywhere it was studded with debris, trees and brush, whole acres of water lilies which here massed like a garden around a floating hut, there wreathed the carcass of some drowned beast.

In all the world there is nothing more melancholy than the voice of a flood. Its resurgent dirge stirs vague forebodings which root in the calamitous experience of the race. Standing there alone, with the call of rushing waters, patter of rain, and sough of a sad wind in his ears, Seyd was able to understand the peons' superstitious fear. Yet he remained undeterred. The water being far too deep for poling, he made a pair of oars and fitted wooden thole pins in the dugout that evening, and next morning put off by himself on the tangled breast of the flood with such food as he had been able to buy.

Once afloat, he found navigation even more precarious than the direst prophecy of his host. Now backwatering until an opening showed in a bristle of brush and water lilies, he would next almost crack his back in a supreme effort to cross the currents which ran like millraces between wooded islands. Once a quick spurt saved him from disastrous collision with a derelict log; and, dodging or running, he was kept so busy that Billy's sudden hail came as a surprise.

"Hello, Seyd! Got any decent grub? We've lived on frijoles straight for the last thirty days."

The monotonous diet, however, did not seem to have impaired Billy's customary cheerfulness. At the sight of eggs, honey, chickens, and bananas in the stern of the boat his freckles loomed like brown spots on a shining sun. Neither had misfortune affected his industry. Though—as Francesca feared—ten feet of water now covered the new foundation, he had immediately started another on a bench which rose fifty feet above the flood. And, now munching a tortilla rolled in honey, he led the way to where Calixto and Caliban, with half a dozen others, were hard at work. It was their first meeting since Seyd left for the States, and there was, of course, no end to the things each had to tell. Then, in reviewing the new work and planning for more, the day slipped rapidly away.

Indeed, afternoon was drawing on before Seyd pushed off again. He had intended to land as close as possible to the inn and have the dugout carried back upstream the following day. But he could not, of course, foresee the event which, a third of the way across, caused him to stop rowing and stare with all his eyes. For as he backwatered to avoid a huge ceiba that bore down upon him with a slow, leisurely roll he spied a patch of white amidst the branches, and as it drew closer this presently resolved into a drenched chemisette which clung to the limbs of a young girl.

A slim brown thing under thirteen, terror had drained away every particle of her natural color, leaving her big dark eyes looming dead black in the pale gold mask of her face. Though she had seen Seyd first, the inborn humility of her subject race deterred her from making any outcry. She just sat perfectly still astride the thatched peak of a submerged hut which, caught in the branches, acted as an outrigger to keep the great tree on an even keel. Only her eyes expressed the pitiful appeal whose utter hopelessness was emphasized by flash of wonder when Seyd drove the dugout in among the branches.

Rising, then, she leaped into the bows, and, whether because the mass rode in a balance too delicate to endure the sudden change of weight or that a submerged branch happened to catch just then on some obstruction, the tree rolled heavily upon the dugout while Seyd was pulling his oars. Fortunately, the one heavy stroke had carried them out from under all but the thinner branches, and, though the dugout was capsized and forced under, it rose instantly, with Seyd and the girl clinging at each end. The hut on which she had been floating also emerged, and, working alongside, Seyd was able to right his craft and bale it out with his Stetson sombrero. A few yards away he recovered one oar, and, using it as a paddle, he tried to work across the flood.

By the time he had gained half the way, however, he was miles below the inn, and dusk found him floating on the wide lake which now covered the San Nicolas cane fields. Here, where the water ran more slowly, he made way faster toward the shore, and through a leaden dusk he presently made out red twinkles which grew, in another half hour, into the lights and fires of the hacienda. Soon his oar struck bottom, and, using it as a pole, he drove rapidly into a landing.

The night rains had already set in and they came down in sheets which soaked him to the skin and made of the girl, who had fallen asleep in the bows, a dim white nude. She had given him her simple history—how, of the five who were asleep in the hut when it was swept away by a cloudburst, she alone had survived. Utterly tired and exhausted, she did not awaken when he picked her up, and she lay quietly in his arms during the long sloppy tramp across the upland pastures. She was still asleep when, aroused by the baying of his dogs, Don Luis peered down from the upper patio upon their draggled figures.

"*Hombres! hombres!*" Looking up as his heavy bass boomed through the hacienda calling the *mozos*, Seyd caught a glimpse under the portal lantern of Francesca's face in its frame of dark hair through a glittering mist of rain.

The next moment she came flying down the great stone stairs, followed by an irruption of brown maids.

"The *niña*! Oh, the poor *niña*!" Though she was wearing an evening dress of delicate white, she gathered the soaked child into her bosom, and, a center of flying skirts and soft womanish exclamations, hurried her away to the upper regions.

In the longer time required for him to descend, Don Luis subdued his first astonishment, but it broke bonds again when Seyd explained his plight. "You crossed and recrossed the flood? *Por Dios mio!* I would never have dreamed that man could do it and live! You are wet to the skin. Come up at once."

"I had not expected—" Seyd began.

But the old man cut him off at once. "You gringos are difficult folk to please. Surely a dry bed in San Nicolas is to be preferred to a wet night on the river."

Nevertheless he was not displeased. Conferring with Francesca concerning a change of clothes after Seyd was safely bestowed in a bedroom, he expressed his secret admiration. "See you, an enormous ceiba rolls over and sends him and the *canoa* to the bottom, yet he speaks of it with shamed laughter as though of a fault. Also he would have borrowed a *mozo* and horse to travel back to the inn. What a man he would have made for the old wars!"

A *charro* suit, so close to Seyd's size as to be almost a fit, was the best that Francesca, after a voluble consultation with her maids, could offer in the way of change, and, though he experienced modest qualms at the sight of himself in tight trousers and short bolero jacket of soft leather gorgeously embroidered with silver, they undoubtedly brought out qualities of limb which were altogether lost in his usual clothing. If he could have seen the touch of admiration that softened the mischief in Francesca's dark eyes when he entered the living-room, his misgivings might have vanished. But the phenomenon occurred behind his back, and his recent vow against "sentimental fooling" did not prevent him from coloring at her whispered remark:

"You remind me of one Señor Rosario."

Later, he was to spend considerable time trying to appease conscience with plausible explanations of his feeling, to set it down to relief that their adventure had brought her no trouble. But while relief may have entered in, it was principally due to the fact that she had chosen to retie the thread of their acquaintance just where it had been severed by Sebastien's intrusion. Yet, whatsoever its constituents, his pleasant embarrassment did not paralyze his tongue.

"I cannot return the compliment."

Neither could he. With Rosa, the pretty peona, this young lady in foamy white had nothing in common, and Rosa would have certainly felt out of place amidst the luxurious appointments of the room. Ample in all its dimensions, the furnishings had evidently been selected from the garnered treasures of several generations, with such taste, however, that the unmatched pieces made a harmonious whole. The old hangings which excluded the damp night, the old rugs on the mahogany floor, and old furniture lent each other countenance, melted into a rich design. Even the grand piano, undoubtedly the latest addition, was taking the tone of age. Only the bookcases which flanked the great fireplace displayed a modern note, for in them fine editions of English classics crowded the novels and plays of Cervantes and Lope Felix de Vega, Daudet, Flaubert, Anatole France, De Maupassant, competed for room with Spanish and English translations of the modern Russians.

"Her taste," Seyd had summed the room. "Your books?" he asked, with a nod at these astonishing shelves.

"Yes, no one else reads them." She added, with smiling directness: "Or could understand. If the dear mother read French, oh, what a bonfire we should have!"

"And you like them—the Frenchmen?"

"Some—in some things." Her brows arching in the effort for clear expression, she went on: "They know life, and one cannot but enjoy their beautiful style. But"—the delicate penciling drew even finer—"they see only with the eye. They are brilliant—as diamonds, and just as hard, cold. They analyze, dissect, probe life, take it apart, then forget to put it together. Love they see only as passion devoid of sympathy, affection, friendship. Their art is of the senses, their refinement—of manner. Under the veneer they are gross and hard."

To his astonishment she had expressed his own feeling for French literature, and, intensely curious, he went on probing her with questions, in his interest forgetting both his clothes and hunger till Don Luis interrupted.

"Lindita, the señor cannot live on words. The girls are calling dinner."

But after the meal—which was set out with silver, glass, napery, all of the finest, and served by brown maids who moved in and out with the soft stealth of bare feet—they went at their talk again, gleaning in fields of common knowledge while Don Luis alternately smoked and dozed by the fire.

It was a revelation for Seyd, and while he watched the play of feeling over her face, the flow of her soft color, the swift moods of the arched brows, and the lighting and lowering of dark eyes in unison with the change of her talk, his hardy resolution of yesterday—already sapped by his present luxurious comfort—underwent further disintegration.

"After all," he thought, "why shouldn't I run down and see them occasionally?"

Following Don Luis to his bedroom, he arrived at this conclusion, and in his argument with Conscience he reaffirmed it with even greater force. "After all the old man's kindness it would be blackly ungrateful to flout his hospitality."

"No reason why you should," Conscience conceded, but added the unpleasant rider, "providing you don't sail under false colors."

"Of course!" Seyd here grew quite huffy with Conscience. "I always intended to let her know I was married—not that it is necessary. I'm not so conceited as to think that she feels the slightest personal interest in me."

If it were really sincere his belief might have been shaken, could he have reviewed a little scene that was being enacted at that very moment across the patio. After the waif from the floods had been bathed and fed she was put to bed on a couch in Francesca's own room, and, aroused by the brilliant sheen of wax candles on the dresser, she lay and watched with eyes of awe the young lady at her toilet. In her simple sight the dresser, with its big French mirror and gleaming silver appointments, doubtless appeared as the altar before which was being accomplished the marvelous transmutation of a woman into the exact semblance of those angels of light pictured on the stained windows of the church of Chilpancin. From the plaiting of the dark cloud of hair into a thick cable, to the final assumption of filmy white, she remained quiet as a mouse. Francesca had risen to blow out the candles before a small voice rose behind her.

"He said you were beautiful. Could he but see thee now!"

After a sudden start Francesca moved over to the couch and collapsed beside it in a white heap.

"Awake, *niña*? What is this? He said I was beautiful? Who?"

"The gringo señor. When I began to cry for my mother and little Pedro that was drowned with her in the flood he said for me to take comfort, that he was going to place me with the most beautiful señorita in all Guerrero—one that would be kinder to me than my mother."

"And that I will be." Drawing her close, Francesca kissed the small gold face. "But did he really say—No, you shall tell me all about it from the very beginning."

While the tale was proceeding in soft lisping Spanish Francesca's eyes eloquently illustrated its varied course. But their wide horror, moist pity at the drowning of the poor brown mother, suspense until Seyd and the child had climbed back into the dugout, merged in a soft glow at the repetition of his promise. "'The most beautiful señorita in all Guerrero?' Then he could not have meant me."

"*Sí.*" The girl emphatically nodded. "Also he said you would take me into your service."

"And so I will. I shall have thee trained for my own little maid. I shall call thee Roberta, after him, and every night it will be thy duty to speak for him in thy prayers. Are they said?"

"*Sí*, señorita. I said them to the big girl, Rosa, but I will say one now for him—with thee."

Could Seyd have heard the soft voice following Francesca's gentle promptings he would undoubtedly have suffered another onslaught from Conscience. As it was, just to prove his disinterestedness he rose at dawn. Leaving a note of thanks on the table, he went out on a hunt for peons and mules to haul the dugout back to the inn, and, having found them, went sternly on about his business.

CHAPTER XIV

For two weeks thereafter Seyd held fast to his work, suppressing with iron firmness successive vagrant impulses which urged a second visit to San Nicolas. Then having proved to himself his perfect indifference toward Francesca, he rode down one day—strictly on business—to ask Don Luis's assistance in obtaining more men and mules.

"I shall return this evening," he arranged with Conscience, starting out.

He had forgotten, however, to make allowance for the probable action of, in legal verbiage, the party of the second part, for upon his arrival he received from Francesca as stiff a lecture on his folly in leaving the other day in half-dried clothes as ever fell from the lips of an anxious mother. Upon it, too, Don Luis set the stamp of his heavy approval.

"One may do it in the high altitudes, señor, but here in the tropics such carelessness leads to the fever. This time we shall not let you forth till properly fed and dried."

Now while a girl's acceptance of flowers, candy, and other favors may mean anything or nothing, no sooner does she begin to concern herself with a man's health and clothes than the affair becomes serious, for it clearly proves that she has been touched in the mother instinct, which forms the basis of woman's love. In his masculine ignorance of this fundamental truth, however, Seyd gave her solicitude a sisterly interpretation, and congratulated himself upon the fact that their acquaintance was established at last on such solid ground. Agreeing with himself that it would be the worst of taste for him to disturb a purely friendly relation with any reference to the squalid tragedy of his marriage, he continued silent.

It is to be feared, also, that several subsequent visits were based upon rather frivolous excuses. In the next month he carried down to San Nicolas the news of at least a dozen cases of destitution through the floods, and when, for some inexplicable cause, deliveries of his material at the railroad suddenly ceased he plunged head over heels into the relief work which had been instituted under Don Luis's direction. Sometimes alone, more often with Francesca and Tomas, he rode up and down the valley hunting out the sufferers. And it was on one of these journeys that the fates which dog insincerity laid bare his pretense.

It came—his awakening—a week or so after a sudden fall of the floods foretold the end of the rains. Though the river still ran wide of its banks, most of the ranches with intervening patches of jungle had come again to the surface; and, riding through one of the latter on his way to San Nicolas, Seyd overtook Francesca and Tomas.

"Is it not good to see the fields again?" she greeted him. "The crops will be late this year, but Don Luis says that the yield will be all the richer because of the flood. But the jungle! The poor jungle! It has been swept clean of shrubs and flowers."

It did look most forlorn. Shorn of its luxuriance, the orchids and wild flowers, and all the tide of vegetation which usually flowed everywhere in waves that rose and tossed a froth of green creepers into the tops of the tallest trees, the jungle was now a fat black marsh littered with bejucos which lay in twisted masses like drowned snakes. Edged with draggled grass, still others hung down from the trees, writhing darkly in the wind that had sprung up in the last hour. Taken in all, it was weird, gruesome, a fit setting for the tragedy that lay waiting for them amid the roots of a dead ceiba just ahead. Twisted back and forth by the storms of the last month, the tree now stood in a hole of mud, ripe and ready for the gust that snapped the rotten tap root just as Francesca was riding by.

Without noise the tree inclined, reaching out huge arms above her head. So silently it fell that Francesca never saw it at all, and Seyd, who was riding just behind her, received first warning from the sudden swing of a bejuco across his eyes. Leaning over his horse's neck, he lashed her beast across the quarters. Almost unseated by the wild forward plunge of her beast, the girl recovered her seat and looked back just in time to see him knocked out of the saddle. Had he been struck by one of the main branches, thick as a barrel, both he and his horse had surely been crushed down into the mud beyond need of other burial. But though he had gained almost from under, even a twig strikes a shrewd blow after describing a three-hundred-foot arc, and he lay in the mud under her eyes, white and still, with an ugly bruise showing across his brow.

"Tomas! Tomas! Ride thou for help!"

Crying it, she leaped from her horse, sank beside Seyd in the mud, and lifted his head into her lap. With water from a pool which was soaking her skirt she laved the bruise with one hand, intently studying his face; and when, some minutes later, he gave no sign of life, her dark anxious eyes blazed with a sudden passion of fear. Gathering his head in against her bosom, she rocked back and forth with passionate murmurs: "Oh, he is dead! He is killed—for me!" But though, if told of it, he would have sworn that such treatment would really have brought him back from the dead, he neither felt, saw, nor heard the soft cradling arms, burning black eyes, the broken murmurs in English and Spanish.

He did feel her lips when, stooping suddenly, she kissed the bruise, because it happened just as her lowered face hid the first quiver of his eyelids. Also he felt the unconscious embrace and saw the deep blush which told that she knew he had felt her kiss. But she did not try to avoid his gaze. From the midst of her blushes she answered it with the bravery of love, discovered and unafraid.

"*Querido*, I had thought thee dead."

In the wonder of it, the foolish, tender wonder, Seyd, on his part, forgot all else. Perhaps the delicate brain plexuses which govern memory were still stunned, leaving his mind clean as a new slate till some stimulus should presently rewrite upon it the pretty, common face of his wife. Conscious only of this new bursting love, he reached up at her murmur and pulled her face down to his. Then it came, the stimulus. With the powerful association of some other kiss, the moist clinging of her lips started the wheels of memory, but, remembering, he did not desist. For simultaneously there had burst upon him a vision of love, rounded and complete, with the perfect fullness which satisfies every instinct and need. Already he had felt that at every point her personality met and complemented his, and in the fullness of the realization his whole being rose in rebellion against that other tie. He was kissing her with furious abandon when she suddenly broke away.

"Oh, I wonder if he saw us?"

Looking quickly up, he saw Tomas returning through the trees. "I don't know," he reassured her, "but I'll find out. If he did—just leave him to me."

After Tomas, but at a safe distance, came three peons whom he had called from the nearest rancho, also a *mozo* who had been sent out from the *meson* to overtake and deliver a letter to Seyd.

"If you'll permit me?" he asked. But his head still swam; and when he tried to read it the angular chirography danced under his eyes, describing such curious antics that he was driven at last to ask her aid.

It was from Peters, the station agent, and announced the arrival of a consignment of American provisions; and, as Billy had been condemned to straight Mexican diet for the last two weeks, the news called for Seyd's instant return. While the soft voice was reciting its content he oscillated between mixed feelings of chagrin and relief, for after its long sleep outraged Conscience was now working overtime. He felt like a hypocrite when she spoke.

"You are still weak. You must not go."

"I'm afraid that I shall have to."

"But suppose that you are taken ill on the way?"

"The *mozo* will be with me—anyway, I'm all right."

Though she looked disappointed, she gave way when he explained Billy's need; the more readily, perhaps, because she felt within her the stirrings of the feminine instinct to hide and brood over her new happiness all alone. The feeling even formed her speech. "The poor señor Thornton! He must be very lonely over there all by himself, and he must be fed. I shall not mind—for a few days. You have given me—so much to think about. But then—you will come?"

He groaned inwardly at the thought of that which their next meeting entailed, and had it been possible he would have preferred to make open confession there and then. As it was not, he let her ride away with her own clear happiness undimmed, unconscious of the stab inflicted by her last tender whisper.

"Surely I shall come," he had answered; and, after mounting his horse, he sat and watched her ride away among the trees. When, with a parting wave, she disappeared, his sun went out, yet through his bitter feeling he remembered his promise.

"Tomas!" He called the *mozo* back. Ignorant of just how much the fellow had seen, he tried him out with the Spanish proverb, "'The saints are good to the blind.'"

At the sight of the five-peso note in Seyd's hand the *mozo's* white teeth flashed in a knowing grin. "*Sí*, señor," he answered in kind, "neither do flies enter a closed mouth." And, pocketing the note, he galloped after his mistress, leaving Seyd to go his own way.

It was not pleasant, either, the path that Seyd pursued the next few days. Going back to the inn, following the mules out to and back from the railroad, crossing and recrossing the river with Billy's supplies, fits of rebellion alternated with moods of black self reproach.

"If you had declared yourself in the beginning she would never have given you a second thought."

Up to the moment when he turned his horse's head once more toward San Nicolas, a few days later, this formed the text of his musings; and if he winced when the gold of the hacienda walls broke along the green foothills it was not in pity for himself. If it would have freed her from pain he would have hugged his own with the savage exultance of a flagellant. But too well he knew that in these things there is no vicarious atonement, and the face that he carried into the San Nicolas patio was so grim and sad that it provoked Don Luis's comment.

"Señor, you are sick? Before she left Francesca told us of the accident. 'Tis plain that you are not yet recovered."

"Before she—left?"

Out of feeling in which surprise and relief struggled with bitter disappointment Seyd's question issued. At Don Luis's answer despair rolled over all.

"*Sí*, señor. She is gone to Europe—for a year."

Through his amazement and despair Seyd felt the justice of the stroke. As yet, however, the smart was too keen for submission. In open mutiny once more against the scheme of things, he repeated the phrase, "Gone? To Europe?"

"*Sí*," Don Luis nodded. "Our kinswoman, the señora Rocha, mother of Sebastien, has been ailing for a great while, and now goes to Europe for special doctoring. As she speaks only our own tongue, she could not journey alone, and, like the good girl that she is, Francesca consented to accompany her."

CHAPTER XV

As a matter of fact, Don Luis knew even less than Seyd of the real reason behind his niece's departure. Like many another and much more important event, it was brought about by the simplest of causes, which went back to the afternoon when, on her arrival at San Nicolas, Francesca found Sebastien waiting there with the news of his mother's illness.

First in the sequence of cause and effect which sent her away stands Seyd's five-peso note; next, Pancho, Sebastien's *mozo*, for the conjunction of these two gave birth to the event. Ordinarily, that is, when in full possession of his simple wits, Tomas, Francesca's *mozo*, would have suffered crucifixion in her cause, and had he chosen any other than Pancho to assist in the transmutation of Seyd's note into alcohol at the San Nicolas wine shop the process would have been accomplished without damage to aught but his own head. But when in the cause of their tipplings Pancho began to enlarge on the benefits that would follow to all from the blending of their respective houses by marriage Tomas began to writhe under the itch of secret and superior knowledge. From knowing winks he progressed to mysterious hints, and finally ended with a clean confession of all he had seen that afternoon.

"But this is not to be spoken of, *hombre*," he warned Pancho, with solemn hiccoughs, at the close. "By the grave of thy father, let not even a whisper forth."

As being less difficult to find in a country where parenthood is more easily traced on the feminine side, Pancho swore to it by the grave of his mother. But, though he added thereto those of his aunts, grandmother, and entire female line, the combined weight still failed to balance such astonishing news. Inflamed by thoughts of the prestige he would gain in his master's sight, he moderated his potations. After he had seen Tomas comfortably bestowed under the *cantina* table he carried the tale straight to Sebastien's room.

In this, however, he showed more zeal than discretion, for in lieu of the expected prestige he got a blow in the mouth which laid him out in a manner convenient for the quirting of his life. Not until Sebastien's arm tired did he gain permission to retire, whimpering, to his straw in the stable; and next morning both he and Tomas trembled for their lives when Sebastien arraigned them before him.

"Listen, dogs!" He struck them with his whip across their faces. "For this piece of lying the tongues of you both should be pulled out by the roots. If I spare you it is because until now you have both been faithful servants. But remember!" He swore to it with an oath so frightfully sacrilegious that both shrank in anticipation of a bolt from the skies. "But remember! If ever, drunk or sober, there proceeds out of either of you one further word 'twill surely be done."

Leaving them shaking, he passed out and on upstairs to the patio where Francesca was sitting, with Roberta at her knees, in the shade of the *corredor's* green arches. The drone of hummers, fluting of birds in the patio garden set her soft musings to pleasant music, and she looked up with sudden vexation at the jangle of his spurs.

"So this is the child that we have renamed in his honor?"

Last night they had parted better friends than usual, for out of the pity bred of her own realized love she had done her best to please him. Love had also sharpened her naturally sensitive perceptions. Divining his knowledge from the concentrated anger of his look, she rose, instinctively nerving herself for the encounter.

"Just so." He divined, in turn, her feeling. "Between those who understand words are wasted. Send the child away."

As he said "understand" a surge of passion wiped out the weary lines left by a night of hate. But while the child was passing along the corridor he controlled it and became his usual sardonic self. He was beginning "Thanks to the excellent Tomas—" when she interrupted with an angry gesture.

"Then it *was* he! I'll have him—"

"*Caramba!*" He shrugged. "What a heat! But easy—do not blame Tomas for your gringo's fault. What else could you expect from a peon that found himself enriched at a stroke? The wonder is that he did not proclaim his news from your topmost wall. Be content that he will never whisper one word again."

"You didn't—" she began, alarmed now for her servant.

"No. Pancho, to whom he told it, I flogged for the liar he now thinks Tomas, and Tomas—is trembling for his tongue. Except between us the matter is dead. Yet Tomas served his purpose. Thanks to him, we may now pass words and come to terms."

"Terms?" She faltered it after a silence.

"Terms!" he repeated, gravely. "That is, if you would save your gringo alive. Supposing this were to escape to the good uncle? Soft as he has been with these gringos of late, supposing that he were to hear of both this and that other night in the hut, how long, think you, would the man last?"

Her eyes told. After a pause her mouth opened with a small gasp. "You— oh! you will not?"

"Not if you obey. Now see you, Francesca." He dropped into a tone of grave confidence which was really winning. "If I had not known that his death at my hands would place you forever beyond me the man had never seen the dawn of another day. Whether he sees its setting depends on you. If you will go with my mother to Europe—"

"*Si*—if—I—go?" It issued between pauses of pain after a long silence.

"He lives. I will even protect him till he arrives at the end of his fool's rope."

"And—then?"

"There will be no 'then.' I know these gringos. They will disappear like their vanishing gold."

Her slight flush indicated defiant unbelief. But knowing that this was in deadly earnest, that Seyd's life hung by a hair, she let him go on. "Let there be no misunderstanding. I shall require your promise, on the word of a Garcia, not to attempt communication." He added, turning away, perhaps in pity for the misery of her face: "There is no hurry. Take time to think it over—an hour, two if you wish."

He could easily afford, too, the concession, for her love was playing into his hands. None knew better than she that a contrary answer would make of Seyd an Ishmaelite with every man's hand raised against his life. He could never escape. With that dread fact staring her in the face she could give but one answer; and while, later, she spent hours pacing her bedroom in restless strivings to find a way out, she reached her decision before he gained the end of the gallery.

"I will go."

CHAPTER XVI

"

Really, I don't know what to make of it. That last car load of machinery rusted for a month in the damp heat of the Tehuantepec tropics before we got it traced. It has happened so often now that I'm almost tempted to suspect a design."

Seyd's complaint to Peters, the agent, nearly a year later summed the exasperating experiences which had retarded the building of the new smelter. Beginning before the end of the last flood, the failure in deliveries had multiplied as the work of construction proceeded, until it seemed to Seyd that his material had been distributed on a thousand side tracks by an impartial hand. While two high-priced American mechanics had spent their expensive leisure shooting and fishing he had spent most of his own time tracing the shipments, and now, with the rains almost due again, another month would be required to finish the work.

"You have sure had your share of bad luck." While sympathizing with him, Peters discouraged the idea of premeditation. "You don't know these Mexican roads. Our charter calls for the employment of sixty-five per cent. of Mexican help, and, if you'll believe me, that means six hundred per-cent. of inefficiency. Take this *mozo* of mine. He's been with me six years. But, though I show him the correct way to do a thing a thousand times, the moment my back is turned he'll go at it in some fool wrong-headed way of his own. The wonder to me is not, that your freight goes wrong, but that it ever arrives. Nevertheless, you've had, as I say, your fill of bad luck. If I were you I'd just jump the up train—she's due in twenty minutes—and call on the general traffic manager in Mexico City. He can do more for you in five minutes than I can in ten days."

It was sound advice. Quick always to perceive advantage, Seyd answered, "Give me a ticket."

Because of his isolation, the agent's wells of speech were always brimming, and while waiting for the train he delivered himself of several pieces of news. "By the way, Don Luis went up yesterday to lodge a protest with the government against the dam a gringo company is building across the valley fifty miles north of San Nicolas. It is located just below the Barranca de Tigres, a cañon that drains all the watershed west of the volcano. They have cloudbursts up there, and when one lets go—well, old Noah's deluge isn't in it. When I was hunting jaguar in the cañon a couple of years ago I saw watermarks a hundred and fifty feet up the mountainside. Boulders big as churches were piled up in the bed of the stream like pebbles, and if that dam was built of solid concrete instead of clay they'd go through it like it was dough. Though I'd be the last man to go back on my own folks, I'm bound to confess that we do carry some things with a bit too high a hand. If that dam ever breaks, the wave will sweep the barranca clean between its walls. But, Lordy! that won't cut any figure with the paint-eaters that hedge in Diaz. To secure a rake-off they'd see all Guerrero drown, and I'm doubting that the General's kick will do any good."

Seyd nodded. "No, the times are against him—both in this and his other efforts to hold back civilization. So far, he and Sebastien have succeeded pretty well in checking it here in Guerrero. But it is creeping in around them—some day will flow over their heads. They might as well stand in the path of a barranca flood."

The naming of Sebastien brought the second piece of news. "That reminds me—you almost had him for a fellow traveler. I forwarded a cable message last night that his mother had died in France. I rather thought that he'd be in for this train."

"Then she is coming back?"

Seyd meant Francesca. But Peters misunderstood. "Yes, they've shipped her by a German line that runs to Havana and Vera Cruz. By mistake the cable was sent to another Rocha somewhere up in Sinaloa, and, being a Mexican, he slept on it a week before replying that his mother was there, quite lively and frisky at home. So it arrived here ten days late—long enough to put Miss Francesca and her mother into Vera Cruz. Yes, the señora was there—had just joined them—luckily, for death is too grim a thing for a young girl to face by herself." Just then the train drew into the station, and as Seyd climbed on, he added: "If you could find time to pass the word on to Don Luis he'd surely appreciate it. He puts up at the Iturbide."

Seyd's nod was purely automatic, for the news had loosed once more bitter tides which had lain dormant these last few months under the weight of his business cares. Unconscious, too, of the import that events would presently give to such apparently trivial consent, he nodded again when Peters asked permission to look through a batch of American papers which had come for him by yesterday's mail.

For that matter, it would have been difficult to discern anything unusual or alarming in the spectacle of Peters as he sat in his office after the departure of the train, heels on the table and chair comfortably tilted, while he slit, one after the other, the covers of Seyd's papers. Yet while he smoked and read his way down through the pile he unconsciously but surely prepared the way for the event which was approaching at the top speed of Sebastien's horse. Had he read, or Sebastien ridden, a little faster or slower things had gone differently. But, just as though it had been predoomed and destined, eyes and hoofs kept perfect time. Just as Peters opened Seyd's Albuquerque paper Sebastien walked in.

"Left—an hour ago." Yawning, Peters laid down the Albuquerque paper on top of the pile, and as the train usually ran from two to twelve hours late three hundred and sixty-five days in the year he lent a sympathetic ear to Sebastien's vitriolic curses.

"I can wire for a special," he suggested. "They could send an engine and car down from Cuernavaca in little more than an hour."

"If you will be so kind, señor."

In all Guerrero, Peters was the one gringo with whom Sebastien was on speaking terms, and he now accepted both a cigar and a paper to while away the time. After one glance had shown it to be a gringo sheet he would have cast it aside, but the one word "Mexico!" in scare heads caught his eye. Setting forth the international complications that were likely to come from the lynching of a Mexican in Arizona, it held his interest. He not only read it to the bottom of the column, but followed over to the next page, upon which heavy ink lines had been scored around a local article.

As the heading caught his eye he started, looked again, then bent over the paper and read to the end. For a few seconds thereafter he sat thinking. A stealthy glance showed Peters at the key clicking off the call for the special. Quietly folding the paper, he slid it beneath his coat.

CHAPTER XVII

With Seyd and his cargo of reflections aboard, the train meanwhile puffed steadily up the four-per-cent. grades which carry the railway eleven thousand feet high to the shoulder of the old giant volcano, Ajuasoa. While he stared out of the window the vivid panorama of the hot country, the green seas of corn or cane which surged around white-walled haciendas, the chocolate peons behind their wooden plows, and the pretty brown girls at the stations gradually gave place to volcanic lava fields and gloomy woods of piñon, and these again merged into the innumerable hamlets which spread brown adobe skirts around Mexico City unseen by him.

"She is coming back! She is coming back!" It ran all the while in his mind, and formed the undertone of his conversation with Don Luis in the patio of the Iturbide that evening. When the old man stated his intention of taking the night train down to the Gulf it was only by a powerful effort that Seyd avoided the lunacy of offering to accompany him. All that night he burned in a flame of feeling, and as a consequence he rose tired out and presented such a picture of meekness when ushered into the office of the general manager, one so opposite to the usual fiery mien of the wronged shipper, that the stony heart of the official was melted within him.

"You certainly have a kick coming," he admitted. "A big one, at that. I'll look into this myself, and if you'll please return at four I hope to have news of your freight."

In their passage down through the departments, however, his inquiries soon came to a stop. "So this is the fellow who has been bucking old General Garcia in the Barranca de Guerrero?" he commented to his third assistant; and his further remarks were equally enlightening. "Well, politics are politics, but this has gone far enough. I like the boy's looks, and this railroad isn't going to be used to fight the General's battles any longer. After this, Mr. Chauvez, see that Mr. Seyd gets his freight. Where is that last car?"

The third assistant's shoulders executed the Latin equivalent of "Search me!" At last news, peon "brakies" on the Nacional had been using it as a roller coaster on the mountain grades going down to Monterey. If Providence had intervened before it ran off into the sea Mr. Chauvez opined that it would most likely be found on that city's wharves. All of which, after some clicking and humming of wires, culminated in the manager's report to Seyd at four.

"It seems that your freight was switched by mistake over to Monterey. If you leave it to us"—his stern eye loosed a twinkle—"you'll probably get it sometime in the next six months. But if you'll take these passes for the evening train and hunt it up yourself you can have it tagged onto the train that leaves to-morrow night."

Though the vicissitudes of thirty years' railroading had almost petrified his heart, the organ stirred faintly as Seyd returned hearty thanks. Watching him go out, he even muttered: "It's a damned shame! But I'll take care that he's bothered no more."

More grateful on his part than he had any legal right to be, Seyd would have been better pleased had the passes read to Vera Cruz. Knowing that Francesca must pass through Mexico City on her way home, he would have preferred even to stay where he was. But the thought of Billy fretting himself thin at the mine reinforced his naturally strong sense of duty, and he took the train out that night. And his steadfastness made for his good. During his three days' absence the flame of feeling which was consuming his resolution and blinding his thought burned itself out. The morning after he had seen his car billed through to his own station he rose with his mind clear and a renewed purpose to do the right thing.

"At the first favorable opportunity I shall tell her," he told himself, in the coach going down to the station. With the thought strong in his mind he stepped on the train and—came face to face with Francesca herself.

"Oh! it is *you*!"

"I—I—thought you were already gone!"

While he blushed and stammered confusedly his senses, nevertheless, took cognizance of the fluttering rush of her hands, the happy eyes in the midst of her flushes, other things that answered, without words, several questions which had greatly perplexed him. Whatever the cause behind her long silence, it was neither the resurrection of her racial pride nor, as he had sometimes suspected, her discovery of his marriage. Indeed, her very next words gave him an inkling.

"You must have wondered why I did not write? But I—could not help it." She glanced at her mother, who, with eloquent hands, was telegraphing him welcome from the other end of the car. "I will tell you later—all."

In his surprise and gladness his mind still clung to his resolve, and, nearly as possible, he kept his pact with himself. "I also have something to tell."

She looked up quickly. But his eyes indicated no diminution of the old feeling. Satisfied, she asked, with a little sigh: "The mine? Something gone wrong? You will tell us—now."

The señora, who had caught the last sentence, added her word. "*Si*, for we, you know, are your friends." Making room for him by her side, she punctuated his tale of the summer's mishaps with pitiful exclamations, and comforted him at the end with maternal solicitude. "*Si*, at the first glance I saw it, that you had suffered. But, courage, *amigo*, it will make for your greater enjoyment in the end."

Francesca had taken the seat opposite, and, catching her eye just then, Seyd saw, along with the sympathy and understanding, a gleam of exultation. "You suffered, *si*, but I'm glad for—'twas for me." Her glance said it plainly as words, and he ached to answer it; but, in accordance with the honest course he had laid out for himself, he refrained, and went on talking to her mother.

"Don Luis," she answered his question, "is in the front car with Sebastien— in attendance on our dear friend, his mother."

He knew that he had no part in their grief, and, tentatively, he began, "If I can be of any help—"

Divining his feeling from the pause, she answered at once: "You are very kind. Francesca, poor *niña*, has been under a great strain. 'Twill be a mercy if you will stay here and talk."

Now that her first blushes had died, he could see it for himself. Her smile added the soft confession, "You did not suffer alone."

Under her look Seyd felt his resolution weaken; to save it he looked out of the window, whereupon it gained strength from the thought of his impending confession. But it relaxed again the next time their glances met; and, as love is an anarchist who scoffs alike at law and death, their communications proceeded with alternate thawings and freezings, while, in reverse order, the black lava fields and gloomy piñon gave place to the painted hamlets, pink churches, and villages of huts in green seas of corn. Yet, if a little worse for wear, his resolution held. Indeed, it found definite expression when the train stopped at last at their station.

"I must see you soon!" he said, as they went out. "I have something very serious to say."

Once more she looked up quickly. "We shall be at El Quiss, Sebastien's place, for three days. After that you will find me at home. But do not come alone!" The hasty addition threw more light on the causes behind her sudden departure. "As you value your life—nay, you were always careless of that— promise, for my sake, that you will not come alone? When you go out anywhere take with you at least one man."

"Is it so serious as that?" But he stopped laughing when he saw she was hurt. "There! I promise!"

She paid him, alighting, with a clasp of her hand that left its soft clinging pressure tingling after she disappeared in the crowd of rancheros and hacendados, Sebastien's retainers and friends, who filled the station. His sharp gray eye had already singled out his car on a side track, and while he waited for the agent Sebastien and Don Luis passed, walking behind the coffin.

He was seen, moreover, by them, and after they had mounted and were riding side by side at the head of the funeral procession Sebastien spoke. "Your gringo was at the station."

Don Luis nodded. "*Si*, he came down on the train."

After a silence Sebastien spoke again. "It seems that he has been having trouble with his freight."

Ignoring the subtle suggestion conveyed by the accent, Don Luis laconically answered, "He is not the first."

"But will be the last. Ernestino Chauvez, my second cousin, is in the department of freights. Yesterday he told me that, by special order, there are to be no more miscarriages of this man's freight."

The heavy brown mask refused even a sign. "This had better happened a year ago."

"Then he is near the end of his rope?" Sebastien leaped to the conclusion.

"His first note of hand to me is due next month."

"And—"

Don Luis's massive shoulders rose. "How should I know, *amigo*, what money he has?"

"But if he pay not?"

Again Don Luis shrugged. "Sebastien, how often am I to tell it—that no gringo shall force in on my lands."

In happy ignorance as yet of the significance implied in their conversation, Seyd at that moment was reading and rereading, with incredulous joy, a newspaper clipping which had been forwarded by a friend in Albuquerque.

MRS. ROBERT SEYD, WIFE OF PROMINENT MINING ENGINEER, GRANTED DIVORCE

The content below ran as is usual when feminine enthusiasm over its wrongs has been unchecked by fear of a reply, and in handing down his decision the local Dogberry—who was unaware that the notice of the plaintiff's remarriage would appear in the same issue with his remarks—had pronounced it the most heartless case of desertion in all his experience upon the bench. Reading a second clipping which set forth the marriage, Seyd indulged in a grin. But this quickly faded. Pity and sympathy colored his remark.

"Poor thing! I hope she'll be happy." Self reproach vibrated in the addition, "She was not, never could have been, with me."

With that she passed out of his thought just as she had already gone from his life. His mind leaped to review the consequences. Free! Free! In the first flush of his joy he exulted over the fact that his intended confession was now unnecessary. But later and more sober reflections caused him to shake his head.

"No!" He laid down the law peremptorily for himself. "There's been enough and to spare of shilly-shallying. You will go to her and tell her—all! And if she refuses you there'll be no one to blame but yourself."

CHAPTER XVIII

In the calendar of love days count as weeks, months as years; but, though the following week conformed to this universal law, Seyd managed to extract from its laggard hours his modicum of joy. Following the mules on two trips between the mine and station he lived in a glow of feeling, the natural reaction of his late despair. By turns relief, joy, hope governed his reflections, finally uniting in optimism that drowned his customary caution. Whereas only a week ago he had begun to plan for a trip home to California to raise money to meet their first note he now determined to put it off until he should have seen Don Luis, and then, if necessary, send Billy.

"I'll call on him immediately after the funeral," he said, talking it over with Billy. "If he demands his pound of flesh there'll still be time for you to go north."

This settled, he had gone about his business in happier mood than he had known for many a year. It seemed to him as if the tangled run of his life was beginning to unfold straight and plain. But while he worked, the evil fates which had made such a ravel in his personal skein were equally busy inventing fresh tangles. On the day that saw at once the delivery of the last piece of machinery and the arrival of the first seasonal rain Sebastien and Francesca joined battle at the El Quiss hacienda.

Until, the morning after the funeral, Sebastien called her aside to thank her for her care of his mother she had shown him only the sympathy due his sorrow. But under it resentment still smoldered, and it was fanned to a flame by his accidental expression.

"It was the kinder because I had forced you away. If I can make any return—"

"You can." She filled his pause. "During the last six months I had time for reflection, and the more I thought of it the more I wondered at myself for my easy yielding to your will. It is not that I was unwilling to do that or more for your mother. But to be sent away like a naughty school girl under a solemn vow against correspondence—"

"The price of your consent, you remember, was the gringo's life?" His eye lit with the old saturnine sparkle. "As you see, he still cumbers good Mexican earth."

"You dared not have harmed him in any case."

"No?"

"No." She met without flinching his look of sarcastic interrogation. "Porfirio Diaz will not stand for the killing of *Americanos*. As you well know, Sebastien, he would surely have hunted you down."

"If there had been any to tell? Even your folly would hardly have arisen to that."

"'Twould not have been necessary. If I had warned him, placed your threat on record with his friends, 'twere sufficient. If not, there is still another argument that would have held you."

"And that?"

"The sure knowledge that I would hate you forever."

"Good reasons, both of them." He shrugged. "But you overlook the fact, my cousin, that a whisper in the ear of the good uncle would have taken the matter out of my hands."

"That would not have cleared you—with me. Now listen, Sebastien. I yielded because at the time it seemed the only way, and after I realized my folly I still lived up to my promise. But now I give you warning. Henceforth I shall not permit your interference in my affairs."

"Your love affairs?"

"*Bueno!*" Looking him straight in the eye, she accepted the correction. "My *love* affairs."

"It will not be necessary."

Instead of the violent outburst she expected he stood looking at her, in his eyes a peculiar light half of pity, half vindictive. A trifle nonplussed, she returned his gaze. Perhaps, with feminine inconsistency, she was not altogether pleased by his tame acceptance, for her color rose and one small foot tapped the polished floor tiles. "I am glad you take it so reasonably."

Again he failed with the expected outburst, and her uneasiness grew in correspondence with the pity in his glance. "You mistake me. I said it would be unnecessary. Read!"

He turned and went out, a mercy she appreciated when, after a puzzled glance at the paper he had stolen from Peters, her eye was guided by the heavy ink scorings to the article that set forth Seyd's divorce. At first she hardly realized its import. But when she did—surely the hand that guided the pen had achieved revenge far beyond its owner's blackest hope! Going out, Sebastien heard the paper crackle. Looking back, he saw her standing frozen, eyes wide and black in her mute white face; and, stricken with sudden pity, he softly closed the door.

But he did not go away. He knew her too well. Given her wild Irish blood plus her Spanish pride there could come but one result, and while she struggled toward it within he paced the *corredor* without. When at last she opened the door and came on him there he knew that he had won by the scorn that set her soft mouth in straight red lines. In the dusk of the *corredor* her face loomed, pale and drawn, the eyes red and swollen. But when she saw the deep pity in his stern eyes her own lost something of their hardness.

"You were always kind—and wise." Her mouth quivering, she gave him both hands. "'Twould have made for my good had I listened to you more."

For him it was a perilous moment. The touch of her hands aroused an intense desire to seize and comfort her with kisses. Had he given way to it she would have surely been shocked out of the resolution that had been born of her anger and shame. But the habit of years enabled him to keep the impulse under restraint. She went quietly to the end.

"I am very grateful—I would like to make some return. If we had not grown up together I should no doubt have loved you from the beginning in the way you wished, for you are closer to the man of my girlish dreams than any other I have ever known." She smiled wanly. "He does not exist, my dream man, or, if he did, what use could he have for such a wild, naughty girl as I? So, if you still want me—"

"Want you!" He would have drawn her to him, but she pulled back.

"Not yet! I like you, have always loved you—in a sisterly way. I must have time to change my viewpoint. Give me a month?"

"And then—"

"If you still wish it I will be your wife."

CHAPTER XIX

As before said, the last piece of machinery and the first rain arrived simultaneously at Santa Gertrudis. The break in the summer heat came with a south wind which herded mountainous vapors in from the warm Pacific. All night the rain fell in sheets that set the thirsty arroyos running bank-high and raised the river ten feet. Then, after the pleasant tropical fashion, the downpour ceased, and day broke with a blaze of sunlight over the Barranca.

"Sinbad's valley of diamonds!"

It was Billy's metaphor when he came out with Seyd from breakfast, and, trite as the comparison might be, nothing else could better describe the millions of wet jewels that flashed in the dark mantle of pine above and embroidered the green cloak of the jungle beneath. Yesterday had seen the last touches put on the aerial cable which would be soon dropping buckets of ore into the red jaws of the furnace two thousand feet below. From the edge of the plateau it ran, a streak of silver fringed with glittering rain drops, down and out to the smelter; and when, in the pride of his heart, Billy loosed the brakes the first vibration threw off a cloud of prismatic spray.

"Balanced to a hair! You see, the weight of one full bucket is sufficient to start the chain."

"Fine!" Seyd echoed. "Runs like a clock. Another week and we'll be running steady."

Standing there, watching the buckets sail up and down like great iron birds, they gave themselves up to the joy of accomplishment; as once before, permitted fancy to run amuck through the golden future. And after their hard labors and prolonged anxieties a little self-congratulation was quite in order. If, one way or another, they succeeded in meeting their first note they really could be counted in splendid shape, for their shipments of copper matte would be on the market before the second fell due.

Billy nodded assent when Seyd spoke. "Francesca said they would be home to-day. I think I'll run down there and tackle Don Luis."

Between them were no secrets, and when Seyd rode away an hour later with Caliban at his heels Billy called after him: "And say, old man, have it out with the girl. If she has half the brains I have always allowed her she'll easily see the accidental way in which it all came about."

Though the advice merely restated his own intention, Seyd found it inspiring. Riding down the Barranca staircases, he whistled and sang. While following the trail through the long succession of ranchos, jungle, hamlets, he lived over again that first ride with Francesca. Very plainly he now perceived that it dated his love, that in the pauses of his stealthy study she had ensnared him with her rich personality.

"She got you then," he mused, adding, with a burst of feeling that astonished himself, "And now I'll get her—if I have to take her by force."

Planning and dreaming, he rode along until the sight of the river, flowing swiftly and deep over the San Nicolas ford, broke up his reverie. Only a mile away, on the other side, the hacienda lay in full view, yet it appeared at first as if they would have to turn back. But after nosing up and down the banks Caliban presently flushed a peon and a dugout. With the horses swimming behind, they were ferried over, and rode across the tree-studded pastures, which were still clad in summer brown.

At the sight of the amber walls in their setting of low brown hills Seyd's pulses had quickened, and, interpreting everything by his own feeling, it seemed to him that the dark women who peeped from their doorways, the swart vaqueros, and the slender girls that passed to and fro with *ollas* balanced ahead, all turned faces of welcome. But when at last he reined in before the shut gates of the *casa* he experienced a sudden, cold revulsion. Like so many eyes, the iron studs stared from the oaken face of the door, until the sudden sliding of a hatch revealed the wrinkled visage of Paulo, the Spanish administrador.

With his employer's toleration of the gringo the administrador had no sympathy. Malice sparkled in his small brown eyes while he answered Seyd's question. "As you see, señor, the *casa* is empty. The señora and the *niña*"— he used the family diminutive for Francesca—"are still at hacienda El Quiss. Don Luis? He has gone again to Ciudad, Mexico, to talk with Porfirio Diaz himself about the gringo dam. I do not know when he will return," he replied, further, "nor the señora."

His high spirits dashed to the ground, Seyd sat his horse, oppressed with heavy forebodings, for the disappointment raised vivid memories of the suddenness with which the girl had been snatched out of his life on two other occasions. Sick at heart, he refused for himself the refreshment that the house's tradition compelled Paulo to offer, and spent the hour required for the beasts' feeding in heavy brooding.

From this, however, he roused himself presently to a lighter mood. "After all, the week is only up to-day," he urged. "She might easily be detained beyond her expectations."

At first he thought of leaving a note. But, realizing the formal terms in which it would have to be couched might make an unfavorable impression, he left, instead, verbal regrets. That settled, he had time to think of Don Luis, and, being now on practical ground, came to a quick conclusion. Forgetting all about his promise not to travel alone, he sent Caliban back to the mine while he went himself straight out to the station.

On his arrival there, however—so late that he had to call Peters out of his bed—he was not a little surprised to find that nothing had been seen of Don Luis. It was, of course, easily possible that he had boarded the train at a flag station ten miles up the line that was nearer to El Quiss. But when, next evening, a thorough search of his usual haunts in Mexico City failed to yield sight or sign of Don Luis, Seyd began to grow suspicious. Suspicion developed into a certainty when on his return two days later Peters informed him that Don Luis had taken the up train that very morning.

"He came from San Nicolas, too," Peters added. "I shouldn't wonder if he was there all the time. Looks to me like he's trying to dodge you."

Intentional or not, it left Seyd in a serious plight. A second trip to Mexico City would take three days. Adding two more to get Billy away in the event of Don Luis's refusal of further time, less than three weeks would be left of their month of grace. It was not to be thought of; and, though the afternoon rains were draping the mountains with heavy gray sheets, he rode out to the inn that night. Crossing the river early next morning, he sent Billy away at once.

"You'll have to spend twelve hours in Mexico City anyway," he instructed him, concerning Don Luis, "so you might as well try to find him. If you succeed, no trifling! Get his fist on a written extension. If he doesn't come through—and I have my doubts—chase right on home to California. With the photos of the prospect and plant you ought not to have much trouble in raising enough to cover the note. And the minute you get it wire me credits on Mexico City."

Hardly expecting it, he was not surprised when Billy wired, two days later, that he was leaving that evening for the States. Under the message Peters had scribbled, "Don Luis came in to-day on Number Nine. Go right down and see him."

Half an hour after receipt of the message Seyd and Caliban were again on their way.

For nearly a week now it had rained heavily night and day, and here and there on the bottoms small inundations gave early warning of coming floods. Though the river still ran in its banks opposite San Nicolas, the dugout in which they crossed was swept with the swimming horses half a mile downstream before they made a landing, and it was easily to be seen that another week's rain would cut off travel on that side of the stream.

Riding in to the great square, Seyd's pulses beat a lively accompaniment to the thought: "It is now the end of the second week. She is sure to be home." Yet in the moment of its riotous birth the hope gave place to black misgivings at the sight of the shut house.

His spirits touched zero when the sliding hatch left Paulo's wrinkled visage framed again in the blank oaken face of the door. "Don Luis is still in Mexico, señor." He anticipated Seyd's question.

"But he returned—was seen the day before yesterday at the station."

"At the station, señor? How could that be?" His brown beads of eyes blinked in uneasy surprise; then in an instant the wrinkled mask fell into an expression of simple cunning. "Or, if so, then it must be that he has gone to join the señora and the *niña*, who are still at El Quiss."

She was not there! For the third time he found himself confronted by silence, mysterious and complete as that which had attended her previous disappearances. But, though oppressed by a weight of care, he tried to hide his bitter disappointment from the administrador's inquisition. Once again he spent a black hour while the beasts were feeding. His broodings, riding homeward, shed no light on the enigma. A night of dark thought left him baffled, furious, in good fettle for the news that Caliban gleaned from a passing charcoal-burner.

"Don Luis must have been there, señor, for Benito saw him ride forth this morning. He has gone north to see for himself the gringo dam."

"Oh, he has, has he!" Seyd ground the words out between his teeth. "The old fox! But now I'll chase him into his earth."

In this, however, he had forgotten to allow for the rains which, driving down the Barranca in great wet sheets, caused Don Luis to put in at El Quiss, there to wait in the leisurely fashion of the country until the weather should break and Sebastien have time to accompany him. Arriving at the power plant after two days' wallowing on jungle trails, Seyd found himself foiled once more in their little game of hide and seek.

The trip, however, was not altogether wasted, for the pert young Chicagoan in charge gave him uproarious welcome. "So you're the fellow that has been bucking the whole state of Guerrero! I'm awfully glad to know you, Mr. Seyd, though I'm puzzled yet as to how you managed to hold out. It took a whole regiment of Diaz's *rurales* to establish us here, and if they were withdrawn even now we wouldn't last long."

Also it was worth the labor to see the dam. A huge earthen structure, nearly a hundred feet high, it spanned the Barranca just where the valley nipped in from a wide angle to a passage a quarter mile wide. Behind it a muddy lake stretched as far as the eye could reach, and while standing in the center Seyd recalled and quoted Peters's prediction.

"'Boulders big as churches were piled up in the bed of the stream like pebbles, and if that dam was built of solid concrete instead of clay they'd go through it like it was dough.'"

The Chicagoan, however, laughed at the quotation. "If the devil himself was bowling them I'd defy him to knock off a single chip. She's solid, and the sluiceways allow ample flood escape. Nothing but an earthquake could touch it—a jim dandy, at that."

Nevertheless, while that enormous volume of water hung suspended, as it were, over the valley, Seyd felt nervous. Traveling homeward the next day, he measured with a careful eye the valley floor, and, using last year's high-water mark as a base for his calculations, concluded that only San Nicolas, the smelter, and one or two haciendas that stood on higher ground would escape destruction if the dam should happen to burst. Approaching El Quiss, he noted, in particular, that, standing on level ground, it would surely be inundated.

For some fifteen miles his trail ran through Sebastien's lands, and, climbing in one place over a knoll, it afforded a view of the hacienda buildings across the rain-swept pastures. As, reining in, Seyd watched the faint pink of the walls flash out and fade in the shifting vapors he was seized with a mad impulse to ride in. But his native good sense quickly reasserted itself, for a moment's reflection showed that the intrusion could only result in humiliation for Francesca and himself. The knowledge, however, did not render her proximity less maddening. He was sitting there restlessly chafing when Caliban's voice suddenly rose behind.

"If it were desired to leave a message there is one I know that could place it in her own hands."

Startled, Seyd swung in the saddle. He had known long ago that kindly usage had transformed the hunchback into a faithful friend, but he was not prepared either for the sympathy that softened his glittering beads of eyes or his uncanny divination.

"*Sí.*" The hunchback nodded. "A cousin of my woman is in Don Sebastien's household service. 'Twould be easy to pass a paper by the little maid you picked out of the river. The señorita keeps her always close to her own body."

Before he finished Seyd had cut a pencil and was writing on the back of an envelope under cover of his raincoat. At first he gave free vent to his feelings, but, remembering the danger of interception, he tore it up and wrote instead a humorous protest against her continued absence. Then, after instructing Caliban to take all the time necessary to procure an answer, he journeyed on alone.

It was well, too, that he gave the hunchback free rein, for three days elapsed before he returned to the mine soaked to the marrow by the continuous rains that had raised the floods almost to last year's mark. "With Don Sebastien one goes slowly," he explained. "If the sharp eye of him had once touched me 'twould have been a short shrift under the nearest tree. For two days I lay close in the *jacal* of my woman's cousin before she brought me this."

It was a considerable package, and Seyd rather wondered at its size while tearing away the dried corn leaves in which Caliban had wrapped it. When the last leaf fell off he stared at first in surprise, then, as his eye fell on the ink scores, in utter consternation at the Albuquerque *Times*. Minutes passed before he could command words to send the hunchback away, then, sitting down by the table, he leaned his head on his hand and remained for some time plunged in black reflection.

From a long distance in time and space his first insincerity had come home to roost. But, while he saw himself as the designer of his own undoing, he was by no means resigned. Presently hard, mutinous lights broke in his gloomy eyes. The stubborn fighter awoke. Throwing the traitorous sheet across the room, he picked up a pen and began to write.

Wasting no time in wonder at the fortuitous chance that had placed the paper in Francesca's hands, he wrote steadily on the story of his love from the first doubtful beginnings to its actual consummation. Very clearly he explained his first natural dislike to intrude his personal affairs upon people for whom he had no reason to suppose they would have the slightest interest, the later honorable intention that had always been frustrated by unfavorable circumstances. And he finished with a statement that is never unwelcome in a woman's ear:

"No matter what comes I shall always love you."

Steady rain all that day and night had given the floods another lift and sent the river roaming wide through the jungle. Once again the valley opposite the mine was converted into a great lake dotted with wooded islands between which swift currents hurtled floating debris. Profiting by last year's lesson,

Seyd had had two roomy dugouts fitted with oars and rowlocks, and early the next morning he rowed Caliban across himself. Returning, he was to send a smoke signal to call the boat, and when, on the afternoon of the fourth day, Seyd spied the thin blue spiral through a break in the drifting rain he almost cracked his back rowing across the flood.

But his glowing hope died at the shake of the hunchback's head. "The señorita is gone with her mother and Don Luis to San Nicolas, señor. But she is to return to El Quiss in a few days. The cousin of my woman had it from Roberta, the little maid. She is still there, and will deliver the letter when the señorita returns."

The news was not altogether bad, for Francesca, at least, was now at San Nicolas. Within the hour Seyd crossed the river to the inn—where a horse was to be had for hire—and his purpose gained strength from a wire that he found waiting there from Billy.

"San Francisco burned to the ground. Not a cent to be raised in California. Am going east."

In view of the aforesaid game of hide and seek he had been playing with Don Luis the situation looked very dark. But, serious as it was, when, halfway to San Nicolas, he met Paulo riding at the head of a mule train loaded with fagots it was wiped altogether out of his mind.

"We go to build beacons along the rim of the Barranca to give warning against the bursting of the gringo dam," he answered Seyd. "*Sí*, Don Luis and the señora are at the *casa*. The señorita?" His creases drew into a malevolent grin. "The señora, you mean. She was married two hours ago to Don Sebastien."

CHAPTER XX

"

What!" In the language of the good old romances, Seyd roared the word.

In the main, Paulo was not a bad old chap. To further the interests of a Garcia he would cheerfully have surrendered his old bones to be boiled in oil, and in his joy at the event he allowed his natural garrulity to dominate his prejudice against the gringo.

"*Si*, señor, they were married at the hacienda by the priest of Chilpancin. On account of the death of Don Sebastien's mother Don Luis and the señora only were present, and immediately afterward the young couple went home alone to El Quiss. A sensible practice, say I! When young hot blood mixes it should be left to cool and settle. Over there at El Quiss the fur will be flying before the end of a week, and put me down as a liar if Francesca do not keep him busy. She has run too long single not to kick at double harness. But she'll settle to it, and like the fine wench she is, there is to be no European travel or such kickshaws as now are common with our rich young folk. No, in the good old Mexican fashion she goes from the church straight to her man's home, there to stay till the first babe makes us all completely happy."

Over and above his real joy in the event the old fellow was undoubtedly aware of its effect on Seyd. While speaking, his small red eyes searched his victim's face for the pain beneath its confusion. But even under the spur of race hatred his imagination could not divine a tithe of the torture he was inflicting. Like all lovers, Seyd had dreamed long moving pictures of himself and Francesca as husband and wife, and now, with the speed of light, the reels spun backward, exhibiting her with another in the thousand and one intimacies of married life. Through all, his stiff Anglo-Saxon reserve persisted, and, finding egress at his heels, the pain that he tried to hide brought the situation to a ludicrous close. Springing from the unconscious pressure of his spurs, his horse, a mettled little beast, collided with Paulo and knocked him flat on his back.

More hurt in his pride than body, the old fellow scrambled up and stood shaking his fist and cursing. But Seyd rode on without attempt to check the animal, whose top speed ran slower than his own hot thought. Indeed, when, from sheer fatigue, it slowed he laid on with quirt and spur, and kept on at a gallop till violent exercise had withdrawn the blood from his swelling brain.

In place of pulsing waves of confused pain came the tortures of clear thought. In turn he was ruled by anger, despair, unbelief. The thought of Francesca as he had seen her on the train, quiet, lovely, sympathetic, inspired the last. It was not possible! Then up would rise the blank ink scores round the divorce notice to provide the motive and plunge him back into deep despair. Lastly came anger, blind and unreasoning, in furious gusts.

Occasionally through his welter of feeling there flashed a glimmer of reason. "She's married now! She's married! That ends it—for you!" But instead of despair the thought produced furious reactions. "I don't care! She's mine! I'll have her—I have to take her by force!" It rose again and again, his cry on the trail of the other day.

By instinct rather than conscious thought he had turned his horse into a path which presently curved at a sharp angle into one that led from San Nicolas up to the rim of the Barranca where at this season ran the only passable trail. At the forks he came on the fresh tracks of shod horses that led up the zigzag staircases.

Overlapping each other on the narrow trail, they might have been made by two or a half dozen, and not until he saw two sets clearly imprinted side by side crossing a small plateau did he think of the riders. If proof were required it was presently furnished by the little handkerchief that hung, fluttering in the rain and wind, on a "crucifixion thorn."

As, reining in, he examined the corner initial a whiff of violets rose in his nostrils. Under the sudden crush of his hand it shed a rain of tears.

CHAPTER XXI

Fifteen miles away along the rim Francesca and Sebastien had just reined in. On a bare knoll close to the trail which led down to El Quiss three peons were building a beacon of dry wood around a core of hay, and while Sebastien talked with them the girl looked out over the valley.

Ever since, in a burst of anger at Seyd's message, she confirmed her conditional promise she had lived in a fever of feeling which precluded clear thought. In the same way that a sufferer from toothache anticipates with almost revengeful pleasure the wrench of the extraction she had looked forward to marriage as though it were to bring the end of her pain. Not until the words that made her a wife fell like a chill on her fever did she perceive the illusion. Riding along the trail, the consequences had presented themselves, and they grew with every mile until they filled her mind with horror. She had shrunk in fear and revulsion when Sebastien offered the ordinary courtesies of the road. When he buttoned his own big rain capote around her she trembled under his hands. Again, when her beast slipped and he threw his arm round her to lift her out of the saddle, she uttered a nervous cry, and, though he released her at once, she shuddered under her cloak. Yet, with all her pain, when she gazed out over the storm-beaten valley her old passion for nature asserted itself through her agony.

Along the Barranca the south wind herded great fleecy clouds. There they piled themselves up in shadowy hills, there they rolled and tumbled like thistledown in a breeze, and again cascaded down to lower levels to dissolve with muttering thunder in slaty sheets of rain. One minute the vapors filled the Barranca, flowing, a ghostly river, between the towering walls. The next a sudden rent in the veil permitted a fleeting glimpse of the trail falling like a yellow snake with myriad writhings into the treetops thousands of feet below. Enormous in scale, the scene was rendered more impressive by the roll of low thunders and flash of pale lightnings amidst leaden writhing shapes. Watching it, Francesca was forgetful until, through a sudden rift, she caught the distant pink flash of the El Quiss walls. Then she shivered, and she was still trembling when, turning from the peons, Sebastien spoke.

"It is one of a chain of beacons they are building up and down the valley to warn the people if the gringo dam should burst." Noticing her shiver, he added: "You are cold, *querida*? Let us ride on."

His usual stern gravity had given place in the last few hours to a look soft, pleasant, and very human. If she had looked into his eyes she might have read there both sympathy and understanding. But softness in him just then merely added to her fear. Following downhill, too, she watched him closely with dark, frightened eyes. In the past his strong face and lithe figure had aroused in her a certain admiration, but now they inspired revulsion. A lost spirit descending into Hades could not have battled more fiercely than did she descending the interminable staircases, and the struggle left her so pale and exhausted that Sebastien remarked upon it when they rode out at last on the valley floor.

"You are tired? We shall soon be there."

That started her again upon a conflict which continued all the way across the pastures to the hacienda gates and reached its climax when she entered her room—not the one she had occupied before, but that which had chambered before her the line of wives and mothers which began with the Aztec bride of Flores Rocha, the conquistador. In that long line the room may have harbored a bride fully as unhappy, but none more mutinous than its present occupant.

"The señora is fatigued. She will have the meal served in her room." Sebastien's quiet order had dispersed the brown maids who flocked about her like cooing pigeons with greetings and offers of service. Unaware that he would observe it himself, she sprang out of her chair and ran a few steps toward the barred window when a tap sounded upon her door. In her relief when it proved to be only Roberta, she pulled the child in to her bosom.

"It is thee, *niña*! Oh! I had thought—what is this?"

Her sudden flush betrayed her recognition of Seyd's writing on the package the girl held out. In the few seconds she stood hesitating her changing expression revealed the struggle between her misery and her sense of wifely honor. The issue was not long in doubt, for, suddenly murmuring "'Twill do no harm to read it," she ripped off the cover.

While she read the blush faded. At the end her low distressed cry, "Francesca, see what thy hasty pride has done! A little patience would have saved thy happiness and his!" told of the deep impression. Sinking into a chair, she was beginning to read it again when the door trembled under a heavier rap.

Thrusting the letter into her bosom, she leaped up, under the urge of the same wild instinct to escape, retreated toward the window, and so stood, with Roberta tightly held against her skirts. Seconds passed before she managed a tremulous "Enter!" and the face she turned to Sebastien presented such a passion of fear, revulsion, and despair that he stopped and stood gazing at her from the door. If surprised, his look, however, was still kind. He even smiled. Not until, retreating as he came forward, she stopped only with her back against the wall, Roberta still between them, did his smile give way to sudden dark offense.

"Are you ill?" He spoke sharply. "Or is this the usual way of a bride? If I were a tiger and you alone in the jungle 'twould be impossible to show more fear."

"I wish you were!" The confession burst out of her miserable fear. "'Twere preferable a thousand times! Oh, why did I do it—commit this great wrong? Love is, can be, the only cause for marriage, but in my hasty pride I sought only revenge—on him. Oh, 'twas a sin—a sin against you, Sebastien, who have always been so kind. Somewhere there must have been a woman who would have borne you children out of her love. And now—I have not only sealed my own misery, but also yours. For, though I do not, never *can* love you, I am—your wife."

To repeat, it came out of her in a wild burst, without consideration. But with the last word she looked her apprehension. He, however, took it quietly. Already the flash of offense had faded. Only the measured tone betrayed restraint.

"It is so—we are husband and wife. But do not let that fact disturb you. Did you think me so much of a beast as to believe that I would take you stone-cold! Neither need you grieve over your sin in marrying without love, for I took you on those terms. I knew very well that you were falling to me through anger. My only fear was that it might cool before you were placed forever beyond the gringo's reach. But now that is accomplished, have no fear, we stand as we were. You are still Francesca, to be wooed with a larger license, but still to be wooed and won to my love."

"Oh, you are—as always—kind!" A little of the terror had died out of her face, and if she had never received Seyd's letter, had lacked the reassurance that lay warm in her breast, his generosity might have prevailed. Pitifully, she was going on, "I am sorry—" but he interrupted.

"Let us have none of that. Pity is the last thing I ask of you. The issue between us lies clearly—can be settled only one way." His dark eyes lighting, he went on after a pause: "It needs not for me to remind you of the birth of my love, for it reaches back beyond your memory. When you were still a lovely child I gleaned a fallen eyelash from your dress and carried it for years—ay, until it was displaced by a stolen curl clipped while you slept by the maid I bribed. With you my love grew—grew with you from that lovely girl into a beautiful woman. The place which your foot had trod was, for me, the only holy ground. You were my church, the only one I ever believed in, the only one that gained my prayers. For me you and you alone held the keys of heaven, and be sure that now that they have passed through your own act into my hands I shall never rest till they have opened for me the doors."

"You will always have my liking and respect—"

He cut her off again. "Idle words—they are not enough. And you owe me one thing—your willingness to help. I shall try hard, harder than I have ever done, to win you, but without that my efforts will be in vain. And remember—for your own sake—if you do not help me it may be that you yourself will reap the pain. The immortality of love is the wild talk of poets. One cannot love a statue. The eye tires at last of the most beautiful marble, goes roving after warm flesh. So take care that you do not awake too late to find yourself unloved, pining for the affection you once rejected."

Through all he had maintained his dark calm, speaking quietly with a touch of sadness. Yet, the stronger for its suppression, vibrant feeling pulsed in the appeal. Had Francesca still been smarting under the lash of hurt pride he might have caught her on a second reaction. For she was moved. Pity and distress governed her answer.

"Oh, I feel wretchedly ungrateful. But what can I do? I cannot—oh, give me time?"

"All that you need, *querida*. You are to have your own time and terms. Now listen! I am going away."

He smiled a little grimly at her start of relief. "So *very* glad? Then I am sorry it will not be for longer. I shall be back in a few days. Word came to the administrador yesterday that the gringo dam is greatly endangered by warm rains that have added the volcano's snows to the flood. A hundred feet deep, the waters are pouring down the Barranca de Tigres, and if they once top it the dam will go." He uttered a bitter oath. "A curse on it! If it were not that the wave would sweep the valley clean I would send one to hasten the end with a charge of powder. But that must wait for the dry season. I go now with every man and mule I can muster to raise and strengthen it. Signal beacons such as we saw at the trail head have been built all along the rim, and, if the dam goes, smoke by day or fire by night will flash timely warning. But if you are timid—San Nicolas stands on higher ground. If you would prefer to return—"

"No! no!" Her fervent gratitude prompted her to attempt some return. "I shall stay here—to care for our people."

He smiled at the "our." "Spoken like a Rocha. You never lacked courage, Francesca, but be careful. At the first signal leave everything, fly with the people up to the hills. If it should happen that the place is spared you can come back again. If not, follow the upper trail down to San Nicolas."

Her fright had now altogether faded. While he was giving a few last instructions a touch of anxiety diluted her brimming thankfulness. But when he went out without having attempted anything more intimate than his usual bow, this vanished. And his restraint gained him more ground. Walking to the window which overlooked the patio, which was now thronged with a motley mixture of peons, mule-drivers, and serving women, she watched him mount and ride away at the head of the mule train. Looking backward from the great gates, he saw and answered the wave of her hand. But it was too far for him to catch either her wistful expression or pitiful murmur "If it had not been—"

Inside her bodice Seyd's letter crackled under her hand. The blush with which she withdrew it indicated a doubt that his letter had a right to further tenancy in that warm nest. Roberta had followed Sebastien out to watch his departure. After placing the letter on the table she sat, one oval cheek propped on her hand, her dark head drooping over it like a tired flower. Once she made to pick it up, then snatched back her hand as though from a flame.

"No! no! It would be wrong—after his kindness." After a few minutes' further musing she added: "'Tis now of the past. By your hand was it put there, Francesca. Now remains only to make a finish."

Taking a match from a tray at her elbow, she lit the letter and threw it, all flaming, to the center of the tiled floor. While its pages withered her face quivered in sympathy, and when suddenly a single line stood blackly out in the expiring glow—"I love you—shall always love you!"—her breath came in a sudden sob.

Rising, she gathered the ashes into a small tray, carried them across the room to the little altar that stood against the wall—an action significant as it was conscious. Kneeling, she bowed her head in her hands. She remained there a full hour, and when she rose no one of the ten generations of women whose soft knees had worn a depression in the tiles was ever animated by a more honest sense of duty. The face she turned to little Roberta, who came bursting in a few minutes later, was quiet and serene.

"Oh, señorita!" In her excitement the child gave her the maiden title. "Pancho, the administrador, will have you come at once. Smoke is rising northward along the rim. Also there comes a horseman at full speed." Lowering her voice, she added: "Pancho showed him to me through Don Sebastien's far-seeing glasses. It is the señor Seyd."

CHAPTER XXII

Riding at a hard gallop, Seyd had cut down Sebastien's lead by a full hour in the run along the rim. At the sight of the beacon—which the peons were now thatching with grass—he, also, reined in. But, having learned from them that Sebastien and Francesca had passed two hours ago, he rode on down the staircases at a pace which showed little respect for his neck.

Nearly an hour later he stopped again on the very knoll from which he had overlooked El Quiss. If he had looked northward it would have been possible to see Sebastien at the head of the mule train which was wriggling like a mottled brown snake across the wet green pastures. But during the quarter hour that Seyd remained there his gaze never left the distant pink of the hacienda walls.

Somehow their solid realism cooled his fever and brought order to his rioting senses. "Well, you are here! Now what are you going to do? What *can* you do?" The still small voice of Reason rose above the storm. "These, you know, are not the days of chivalry. It is no longer the fashion for a jilted lover to snatch his bride from the horns of the altar. And if it were"—Reason here observed a deadly pause—"what chance would you have against Sebastien and his retainers?"

"But I must see her! I *will* see her!" The still small voice was drowned in a gush of passion. "There have been too many accidents already. Not till I hear from her own lips that she has done this of her free will shall I quit."

"Sounds good." Reason agreed only to differ. "But it has one drawback— she might not care to be interviewed in her bridal chamber."

The suggestion was ill-timed, for it started a new riot among his senses. "I'll see her! I *will* have speech with her!" It went roaring through his brain.

But how to compass it? Had he known the name of Caliban's woman's cousin it would have been difficult enough! Not knowing it, the thing was almost impossible. He was tossing on successive waves of feeling that now urged him forward, again carried him back in the undertow of despair, when there came a patter of nude feet behind him.

"Señor! señor! *Mira!* The beacons! The beacons!"

It was one of the peons whom he had left above. "Ride, señor! Ride and give warning lest they have not seen it at El Quiss! I go to my woman and children!" Shouting it, he swung at right angles and flew down the valley at top speed.

Almost as quickly Seyd galloped off. One glance had shown the tall smoke plumes which were rising like ghostly sentinels above the black edge of the pine, and with it there burst upon him a vivid picture of the muddy sea behind the great dam. Crossing the river that morning, he had noticed that the floods were running above last year's highest mark, and almost as plainly as by actual sight his imagination pictured the wave which had just leaped, like a huge yellow hound, over the broken dam. A solid wall of water, he saw it sweeping down the valley, lapping up villages, ranches, *jacals*, with greedy tongues. Roweling the flanks of his tired beast, he drove on. Yet, despite his apprehension, the phrase rang in his mind like a clashing bell:

"I shall see her! Now I shall see her!"

While he was still half a mile away he saw two mounted men dash out of the patio gates and ride off at right angles, north and south. After them came a crowd on foot, and as they opened to let him through Seyd noted with wonder that all were women. His surprise deepened when, driving in through the gates, he almost rode over Francesca, who stood with Roberta against her skirts in the deserted patio. While, breathing hard after his wild ride, he sat looking down upon her she returned his gaze with big mournful eyes.

"You are—alone?"

"Yes." Hesitating, she went on, "Don Sebastien left an hour ago—immediately after our arrival—with the men to work on the dam."

He almost shouted. It was inconceivable, except on a supposition that filled him with sudden hope. "Then it isn't true? If it were, he would not have left you. He lied! Paulo lied! All day I have ridden hard on your trail to disprove it! He lied! Tell me that Paulo lied!"

It was not necessary to reply in words. The slender weaving fingers, her quivering distress, the pity and grief of her eyes, made answer.

"Oh, how could you?" But his natural sense of justice instantly asserted itself. "But no! I have only myself to blame. I played the fool all through. Yet, I meant well—but I explained that in my letter."

"I only received it two hours ago. Oh, why didn't you send it sooner?"

"I did—wrote the instant I got the paper. It lay here four days."

Now, only twenty miles away, at speed swifter than bird flight, the wave was leaping over the jungle with plumage of tangled debris streaming out behind. Even then they might have caught its distant roar. But, blind to all but the fortuitous chance that had dogged their love to this unhappy conclusion, they stood gazing at each other in distress and despair.

"We have been unfortunate, you and I." She spoke, mournfully, at last. "And this is the end."

He would not accept it. In thought he was storming the barrier her act had placed between them when her sorrowful voice answered the mute appeal of his eyes. "*Si*, the end. If Sebastien had not been so kind! He took advantage of my anger to place bars between you and me, but there he rests. His consideration deserves some return, and the least I can offer is the outward semblance of good wifehood. You must go!"

"What! Leave you—now?" Recalled to a sudden realization of their imminent danger, he pleaded, "First let me place you in safety?"

"No." She nodded toward a saddled horse under the gateway. "In a few minutes I can overtake the people. With you will go my—"

While they talked Roberta had wandered over to the gates. Now she suddenly cried: "Oh, señora! Don Sebastien!"

Seyd's view of the trail was limited by a swing to the south that cut off all but a couple of hundred yards. As he made, instinctively, to move forward Francesca caught his bridle. "No! no! He must not see you! If he finds you here—with me—oh, has there not been trouble enough?" Her distracted glance circled the courtyard. "See, the old guardhouse! Dismount—quickly! Lead in your horse, then I will ride with the child to meet him!"

As a matter of fact, he felt like anything but hiding. His eye lit with a hard gray gleam. But in these premises that he had forced upon her it was not for him to pick and choose. He yielded to her pleading, "For my sake?"

Dismounting, he led his horse in through the arched doorway, and as she closed the door upon him Francesca added a last hurried instruction. "He will undoubtedly turn with me. Give us time to gain cover under the oaks, then take you the trail to the south. It reaches high ground quickly. And ride hard"—her voice broke in a sob—"for if you should be overtaken by the water what in this miserable world would be left for me?"

"And this is the end?" He caught her hand between the closing doors.

"The end—for thy sake." She dropped into the tender second person of the Spanish. "*Si*, if you wish it."

Left alone, Seyd stood listening, the soft touch of her lips thrilling upon his. In the guardhouse, used now for a storeroom, all but one window was blocked by piles of sacked maize, but as his eyes grew accustomed to the half gloom he made out the massive beams which held up the heavy roof. The wall from which the one window looked out formed part of the hacienda's southern face, and, remembering that the trail inclined in that direction, he moved over to it when he caught the clatter of departing hoofs. Deeply recessed in the thick wall, the low sill afforded standing room, and by peering obliquely through the bars he caught first the flutter of her skirt, then gradually she forged into full view. About three hundred yards away the trail ran in among shade oaks, cedars, and great spreading banyans, that were strewn in clumps all over the pastures. But just before she rode in among them Sebastien and Pancho, his *mozo*, galloped out from among the trees.

Even if the wind had not been dashing the sheeting rain in his face it would have been impossible for Seyd to have caught a distant murmur of voices. But he saw the *mozo* lift Roberta from Francesca's beast, and lead off, with his mistress following. Then Sebastien came galloping on toward the gates.

"Coming for something—money or papers," Seyd thought. "Just for fear he looks in—"

At the far end of the room a pile of sacked beans formed a natural stall, and he had no more than gotten his horse behind it when the clatter of hoofs broke in the court. He could not, of course, see Sebastien dismount. But, faint as they were, his highly keyed senses recorded the vibrations of the other's footsteps as he followed the muddy horse tracks across to the guardhouse.

Outside the door Sebastien stopped. In the tense pause that followed Seyd's hand went to his gun. At first the act was due to the natural instinct of self protection, but in the very moment of its inception that gave place to a second, more powerful impulse that dyed his face and neck with a dark flush. Drawing the weapon, he trained it across a sack at the door, and at that moment no primitive man in hiding at the mouth of his enemy's cave was ever obsessed by a fiercer lust to kill. All of his trials and long travail, despair, seemed in his disordered fancy to materialize just then in Sebastien's person. And it would be so easy! A slight pressure of his finger the instant he showed in the doorway, then—the flood!

In a flash the pros and cons of it passed through his mind. If the circumstances were reversed he knew exactly the course that Sebastien would take. And almost as he thought it came proof—first the grating of the key in the lock of the inner door, next the groaning complaint of rusty hinges as Sebastien swung to the iron outer doors which had not been used for a score of years, finally the wooden crash of the oaken bars falling into their staples.

It was all over before Seyd really understood. With knowledge there flashed upon him the thought of the flood. Rushing across the floor, he leaped and threw all of his weight against the inner door. It hardly shook, and the recoil threw him flat on the floor. As he rose came the clatter of Sebastien's departing hoofs, and running across to the window he was just in time to see him come in view. On the skirts of the timber he reined suddenly in and sat his beast, listening. Then, after a quick glance northward, he galloped on.

And Seyd, at the window, also heard.

Above the sough of the wind which drove the sheeting rain into his face he caught the roar of the oncoming flood.

CHAPTER XXIII

In the few minutes that passed before she met Sebastien Francesca had regained self control. To his reproof, "This was foolish; why did you linger?" she calmly replied, "I wished to make sure that all the people were out."

He nodded approval. "Then no one is left?"

"No one."

"*Bueno!* We have no more than time to make the hills. Pancho's beast is stronger than yours. Give him the child." She had begun to hope, but it died within her as he went on: "In my rooms are valuable papers. 'Twill take but a moment to get them. Ride on, you. My horse goes two paces to your one. I can catch you halfway to the hills."

She almost fainted when he rode off, for just as surely as though she had seen him questioning the fugitive women she knew now that he was aware of Seyd's presence. She reined her animal around to follow, then checked it sharply under a sudden inspiration.

"Why do you wait, Pancho?" she asked, sharply. "While you sleep the flood will be on us. Ride! Ride your hardest! I will follow."

The *mozo*, to tell the truth, was damning with inward tremblings the luck that had placed him in such jeopardy. Only the fear of Sebastien had kept him from bolting, and now, without even a backward glance, he laid on with quirt and spurs and galloped off with Roberta, leaving Francesca free to carry out her plan.

It was quite simple. In this, the rainy season, the shade trees were draped from crown to foot with green lace of morning glories, and on the outer edge of the nearest clump a banyan had been converted into a huge tent which would have stabled a hundred horses. Parting the lacework of leaves with one hand, after she had ridden under it, Francesca obtained, through the gateway, an oblique view of the guardhouse at the moment Sebastien closed the iron doors. The crash of the bars carried to her tree, and had he looked that way he might have seen the curtain of leaves swing under the forward move of her beast. But, controlling the impulse, she reined it back again. When Sebastien raced past a couple of minutes later she dropped her hand and shrank in sudden fear.

It was, however, impossible for him to see her. Moreover, the intervening clumps prevented him from discovering that she was not with Pancho until he came bursting out on his heels in open pasture half a mile ahead.

"*Tonto!* where is thy mistress?"

The *mozo's* look of frightened surprise proclaimed at once his ignorance and fear. Both had reined in, and under the other's deadly look Pancho cowered behind his bent arm. Sickly green patches stained his dull chocolate. When Sebastien pulled a pistol from his holster he bowed down to the saddle horn, his face in his hands. Leaning over, Sebastien placed the muzzle against the fellow's head. His finger even had tightened. Then, checking the impulse, came Roberta's whimper, "Señor! oh, señor!" Above it rose a distant thunderous roar, and, glancing northward, he saw in the far distance a writhing movement in the jungle beyond the pastures.

"Off, fool! Save the child!"

Striking the man's shoulders with the pistol, he wheeled his horse and shot away, heading back to the hacienda. Riding, he kept one eye on the green wave that was moving with the speed of the wind over the jungle. As he passed in among the shade trees it boiled over the far edge of the pastures, and from beneath the swaying trees emerged a muddy wall crowned with bristling black. Traveling more swiftly in the open, it came on at an acute angle which had its point in the flooded lands along the river, its base in the jungle close to the hills, and when Sebastien dashed out of the timber the point had passed the hacienda.

Even then he must have known it for hopeless. The thunderous diapason had risen into a furious crescendo which was spaced by the tear and crash of uprooted trees, and, higher than his head, the liquid wall was coming on under the pressure of the yellow frothing sea that stretched behind to the limit of sight. Yet, laying on quirt and spurs, he raced down its front in a desperate spurt for the gates.

While he was still a hundred yards away the wave struck the northern wall of the compound that fenced the buildings. Built solidly of stone, it melted, vanished without a premonitory shiver, and in its overthrow accomplished good. Catching root and branch in the debris, the grinding welter of fallen trees hesitated, then piled in a huge tangled bar upon the line of cottages and stables which intervened between the wall and house.

To Sebastien, however, this brought no respite. Shooting along the eastern wall, the wave outraced him and beat him to the gate by a long fifty yards.

While Francesca was still under the banyan she had heard the roaring diapason of the flood. Clothed in dripping lacery of leaves and flowers torn away by the beast's leap from the spur, she galloped into the patio, and when she dismounted the vines still twined around her limbs. Without waiting to tear them off she threw all of her strength into a vain effort to swing the bars of the guardhouse doors, but, swollen by the rain, they were fast in the staples.

"Oh, *what* shall I do?"

Her cry carried through to Seyd. After a fruitless attempt on the door he was just about to attack the window bars with an oaken club he had found in one corner. Now, tearing away the sacks of maize that blocked the one small square window on her side, he thrust it between the bars.

"Knock them up with this!"

But after the bars yielded the rusty doors defied her strength. "They will not budge! Oh, I cannot move them!"

Again his practical sense served. "Slip a stirrup over the staple, then start your horse gently. Fine!" He heard the groan of the moving door. "Key gone! Never mind, I can shoot out the lock. Stand away—off to one side."

Above the roar of the flood Sebastien heard the shots. A few seconds later he saw Seyd look out of the gateway, then rush back in. Behind the gates an iron ladder led up to a lookout post on top of the guardhouse, and, racing down the front of the wave, Sebastien saw Seyd rise above the low parapet and lift Francesca to his side.

At the same moment they saw him. In Francesca's outstretched hands Sebastien saw her impulse to save. In the sudden covering of her eyes he read his fate. The fifty yards that lay between him and the gates might just as well have been a thousand, for, less than half the distance away, the great yellow comber rose high over his head.

Before it broke, however, he did two things—reined his horse to face it, then, just before he went under the grinding welter, with the same easy courtesy which he would have shown to a kinsman or a friend, he turned in the saddle and waved his hand.

CHAPTER XXIV

From the time Seyd rode into the hacienda up to that moment less than twenty minutes had passed, but events had leaped to a conclusion.

The barrier of debris across the outer buildings had diminished the force of the blow upon the house, and had the water gained instant access to the interior and equalized the pressure it might have stood. As the wave raced past, level with the high wall, the patio presented for an instant a curious resemblance to a square vessel pressed down till its edges just rose above the water. The next, its stout walls fell inward, and over them a yellow wave leaped at the house. Reinforced by its partition walls, it withstood for a few seconds the enormous pressure. Then above the cracking and grinding of debris and the mingled roar of the flood rose the boom of doors and windows blown out of their frames.

Because of its length the guardhouse went first. Feeling it tremble under his feet, Seyd lifted Francesca and held her face in against his breast. Not that he was in the least resigned. Never in all his life had he felt a keener desire to live. His glance darted hither and thither, and when, freed by the fall of the stone lintels, a patio gate sprang out of the yellow cauldron almost at his feet he snatched up Francesca, leaped, and landed in its very center. Falling under her, he was, for an instant, breathless. But in the few seconds that he lay there gasping circumstances worked in their favor. Thrust by the impact into the recoil of the wave from the house wall, the gate was heaved out of the patio, and passed the guardhouse just before the heavy tiled roof collapsed with the walls.

Almost in an instant the house crumbled and melted with scarcely a splash. Sitting up a few seconds later, Seyd looked back on all that was left of El Quiss, the barrier of debris rising, a black reef, out of a yellow sea. A mile ahead the wave roared on, its furious crescendo again reduced to a booming diapason. While the gate was being carried with incredible swiftness across the El Quiss pastures the roar sank to a distant hum, and presently died altogether, leaving only the quiet lapping of the waters in the falling dusk.

So quickly had it all passed that Seyd found it hard to believe they were floating in comparative safety. The gate, which was ten feet by twelve in size and four inches thick, floated evenly, and if an occasional wave ran across it the tepid rain water of the tropics caused no discomfort. Neither were they in danger from the debris, logs, and uprooted trees which floated at equal speed on currents that were setting back to the river. With a pole that he picked up Seyd was able to keep out of the way of the few that rolled and tumbled when their branches caught on the bottom, and when at last they drifted on the deeper, slower currents of the river he turned to Francesca, who had remained a huddled, sobbing heap just where she fell.

She looked up when he touched her shoulder. "Oh, I feel wicked!" she cried, remorsefully. "If I had only waited for a few more days, given you time to explain, he would still be alive."

"It was perfectly natural," Seyd comforted her. "He would absolve you from all blame were he here, for with all his faults he was big and brave."

"You really think that he would?" She looked up with tearful anxiety.

"I'm sure of it. How could he do otherwise?"

"But he was—my husband. And I left him—for you."

"Yet I do not think that he held you in blame."

Kneeling beside her, with one arm around her shoulders, he gave his reason—Sebastien's last salute. Even if this started her tears anew she, nevertheless, felt comforted. When a black shape forged out of the dusk alongside, and he had to return to his pole, her natural spirit reasserted itself.

"Here am I, crying like a child instead of helping. What can I do?"

There was really nothing. But to keep her from brooding he placed her on watch. "If you'll keep a lookout I'll take a shove at everything that floats in reach. The current is setting across the river, and we have nearly twenty miles to work in. With any old luck we ought to be able to land at Santa Gertrudis."

Thick dusk presently merged into night, but they were helped by a full moon which shed a dew of light through the falling rain. Not that they voyaged without hazard. Twice they were almost swamped by trees which rolled over under the thrust of Seyd's pole. Farther down they narrowly escaped shipwreck on wooded islands. Yet, thrusting and hauling, he worked steadily with the favoring current, and they had gained almost across when, rounding a bend, they sighted a distant light.

"Caliban's, for sure! Only another hour to food and fire!" Seyd cheered her.

He had, however, his own misgivings. As they drew into the shadow of the Barranca wall the moonlight grew fainter, and, drifting later over the submerged jungle, they were hard put to avoid the treetops which upreared like huge mushrooms above the flood. More than once they were almost swept off the raft by bejucos, vegetable cables, which stretched from top to top, and as these grew thicker Seyd saw that disaster was merely a question of time. He was hoping desperately that their capsizing would not entail too long a swim, when out of the obscurity rose a huge black shape.

With a shock that threw them both down, the raft grounded in shallow water.

It was the plateau on which the new smelter stood. But, changed as it was in the new geography of the flood, Seyd did not recognize it until, scrambling ashore with Francesca, he saw above the dark mass of the buildings the cable and iron ore buckets in dim outline against the sky.

"Why, it's the smelter!" he shouted, in glad surprise. "Ever since the explosion we have kept a man here on guard. *Ola!* Calixto! *Ola! Ola!*"

While he was calling a yellow oblong broke out of the building's mass, framing the black silhouette of a man. "It is the *jefe!*" They heard his comment to his woman inside, then, uttering a volley of surprised "*Caramba's!*" he came rushing down the bank with his lantern.

When Francesca's pale wet face shone under its sudden glow he dropped the lantern, which, fortunately, did not go out. Picking it up again, he lighted their way to the adobe that had served Billy for house and office while the smelter was building.

For use during the rains, a chimney and wide hearth had been installed in the adobe, and while Calixto was building a roaring fire Seyd directed a piratical raid on Billy's trunks. At first his search returned only muddy overalls and soiled clothing of various sorts, but at the very bottom—just as they had been placed by the hands of a careful mother—a new suit of flannel pajamas and a voluminous woolen bathrobe appeared. When, with some misgivings, and confused, he suggested a change, a touch of the girl's old archness flashed out. Her smile was almost mischievous as she returned thanks.

"I'm sorry there's nothing better to offer." The smile emboldened him to add: "But they will serve till we have something to eat. Then you may have the fire all to yourself to dry your own things."

She smiled again when, returning with food and coffee prepared by Calixto's woman, he exclaimed, "You look like the Queen of Sheba!"

With the brown-black hair swinging almost to her knees and the bathrobe— a gorgeous affair in pink chosen with an eye to Billy's vivid taste—belted in to her waist and pajamas ballooning beneath over small bare feet, she did look Oriental. When the coffee and food had relit her eyes and restored her usual faint color he was sure that she had never looked so distractingly pretty. The effect was not diminished either by her small vexed frowns at the revelations of smooth whiteness caused by the persistent slipping of the wide sleeves. When, as they sat by the fire after the meal, warmth and fatigue moved her to a yawn and he caught the full redness of her mouth before she could cover it the intimacy of it all sent the blood drumming through his pulses. If her serious eyes restrained him, they did not repress his thought.

"I have you—now! I have you at last, and I'll never let you go again!"

Undoubtedly she furnished the inspiration which kindled a sudden light in his eyes. "Why not?" he urged against the one objection that occurred in his thought. "It's an awful smash at the conventions, but—it's the only way. He locked me in to drown—and do you suppose that he'd hesitate if he were here now in my shoes? I guess not. And if he would, I won't. By the Lord, I'll do it!"

He rose soon after reaching his conclusion. "You must be very tired, so I'll go now and leave you to dry your things. You know, we start early in the morning."

"Start early?" She opened her sleepy eyes.

"Listen!" He took her gently by both shoulders. "We have been held apart so far by all sorts of accidents and misunderstandings. You know how closely we came to utter shipwreck?" Her shiver answering, he went on, "Now, will you trust—leave all to me?"

She had been no woman if she had not divined the restraint behind his quiet during the last warm hour, and, rising suddenly upon small bare toes, she paid him for his consideration. "I will do anything you say."

CHAPTER XXV

Breaking through the stream of ocean vapors, the morning sun showed the jungle raising a languid head above the ruins of the flood. Long rents in its green mantle, bare patches of yellow mud, dark bruises where acres of debris had been piled in twisted masses, testified to the force of the wave. But, overlooking the wreckage from the smelter, Seyd took notice principally of a fact that suited his purpose—the river had been swept clean of driftwood. Not since the beginning of the rains had it shown such open stretches.

"Good!" he muttered. "The sooner we get away the better. I'll call her at once."

When, however, he knocked at the office door Francesca answered "Come!" When he entered she smiled at his surprise. "You said that we were to start early. Here I am, dressed and dried."

"Not before breakfast," he laughed. "It is ready. I'll have it brought right in."

All through the meal her eyes questioned, but, denying her curiosity, he talked of anything and everything but that which filled her mind. Even when, clothed in his waterproof, she took her seat opposite him in the stern of the dugout he denied their eloquent appeal. While sending the boat with vigorous strokes flying downstream he drew her attention to this and that phase of devastation and commented on the beauty of the morning, but not a word as to his purpose. It was cruel, and her eyes said so. But, remorseless, he held on till, about midway of the morning, they sighted San Nicolas. All the way down he had hugged the Santa Gertrudis side, and she received the first inkling when he replied to her question if it were not time to pull across.

"We are not going there."

"Not going there?" she repeated, surprised.

"No, we shall keep right on—down to sea."

"The sea?"

"The sea." He nodded firmly. "And the minute we land there we're going to be married."

The idea was altogether too radical to be absorbed at once. No doubt she thought he was joking, for a smile broke around her mouth. Not until they were almost opposite San Nicolas did it give place to puzzled alarm.

"But, señor—Rob—Roberto." She changed it in answer to his quick look. "But, Roberto—"

"Might as well make it Bob," he cut in, crisply. "It may seem strange at first, but seeing that we're to be married you might as well begin to get used to it now."

The San Nicolas walls now lay, a long, warm band, across their beam. From them her glance returned to the pendulum swing of his body. Finality centered in his steady stroke. It told that he had settled down for the day. Had he calculated its effect beforehand he could not have done better. Accustomed to Spanish deference, she was nonplussed by his authoritative air, yet its very unusualness invested it with a certain charm.

"But—Bob?" Somehow the curt appellation acquired grace and softness from her Spanish lisp. It fell so prettily that he made her repeat it. But, though she added to its attraction an appealing glance, he remained grimly obdurate.

"Give me time to think?"

"All you want. At this speed"—the oars creaked under his stroke—"you will have about twenty-four hours."

She looked at him, frightened. "*Please?* At least let us talk it over."

The cheerful roll of oars in the rowlocks returned wooden answer.

"Won't you?"

He stopped rowing and sat regarding her sternly. "I'm allowing you more time than you gave me. If"—he paused, then, judging it necessary, relentlessly continued—"if *he* were here in my place do you suppose—"

"Oh, he would! He did! After he had insured me against—"

"—Me," he supplied, with a dogged shake of the head, then went on, "Well, even if he would, I won't." As he bent again to the oars the touch of admiration that leavened her undoubted fright paid tribute to his stubborn logic. Settling to his stroke, he began again: "Supposing that I complied and put you ashore at San Nicolas? Do you think that Don Luis would be any more favorably inclined toward me? You know that he wouldn't. I should do well to escape with my life. But if you go back as my wife—well, the most they can do is to turn us out. Of course I can understand your feeling. It will be a frightful breach of the conventions—"

"No, it is not that," she interrupted him. "My friends will be scandalized, *si*, but they are long ago broken to that. They would be dreadfully disappointed if I did not fulfil their predictions by making a shameful end. And it isn't— he. It is wicked to acknowledge it, but I know—I know now that no matter how hard I tried to school myself I should sooner or later have run away to you. They'll think it shocking—my friends, my mother—but I can endure it."

"And that can be avoided. I'll take you away—throw up everything here—make a new start somewhere else."

"No! no!" She shook her head. "Your work is here, and I am just as proud of it as you could be. Let them chatter. No, it isn't even that."

"Then what is it?"

"You wouldn't understand. It is silly, just a woman's reason. No, you would not understand."

"I'll try."

"It is *so* foolish." Nevertheless, encouraged by his sympathy, she continued: "Do you know that since the first kiss passed between us a year ago we have had speech together only for a few minutes in the presence of others? And her courtship is of such supreme importance in a girl's life. It is her love time, and she loves to lengthen and draw out its lingering sweetness. And ours has been so short."

It was the poignant cry of her girl's heart expressing the yearning of her starved love, and, coming from such spirited lips, it moved him deeply. Slipping the oars, he seized her two hands and pulled her forward into his arms. Then, while her dark head lay pillowed upon his shoulder, he continued the argument to better advantage.

The walls of San Nicolas had dwindled to a golden streak before she looked up in his face. "Supposing that I had refused?"

"I'd have carried you off in spite of yourself."

And, whether she believed him or not, she clung the closer in that embrace.

CHAPTER XXVI

The new day opened a new and fertile country before Seyd's sleepy eyes, a country wonderfully beautiful with variegated foliage of coffee, rubber, palm, and banana plantations.

During the night the Barranca walls had, while growing lower, closed in to a long gorge through which the river ran like a millrace. For two hours their ears were dinned and deafened by the roar and thunder of mad waters, but, as the boulders of the one rapid were buried thirty feet deep, they sustained nothing worse than a slight deafness and natural apprehension at the hair-raising speed with which they were catapulted onward. Excepting those two hours when he had to use both oars to hold the dugout's head in the center of the current, Francesca had slept in his arms, and, nestling upon his shoulder the moment they emerged upon quieter waters, she had fallen asleep once more, nor did she move till the sun pointed a golden finger down between two clouds.

Awakening, she uttered a small cry and lay for a few seconds looking up into Seyd's face, her eyes blank with bewildered terror. Then, recognizing him, she gave a sob of relief. "Oh, I was dreaming—that I was at El Quiss—to stay there—forever!" She paused and sat for a moment looking into his tired face, then burst out: "Oh, little animal! All night I slept while you kept watch. Now you shall sleep."

Taking his place in the stern, she forced him, with pretty authority, to cushion his head in her lap. "*Si*, I will awaken you before we reach the harbor, but do not dare to open an eye till then."

The command was unnecessary, for, completely fagged, he had no more than lain down when he was fast asleep. Until sure of the fact she sat perfectly still. Then, with a rueful glance at her soiled and shrunken garments, she murmured, "Nevertheless, we must try to look our best."

After a second shy study of his sleeping face she let down her hair and began to comb it out with her slender fingers. Because of the length and thickness of the dark masses this proved a long task. The dugout had drifted miles before she finished the coiffure with small feminine pats. Reassured that he still slept, she dipped her handkerchief overside and washed her face and neck.

Her own toilet completed, she next essayed his. After warming the wet handkerchief against her own cheek she cleansed his face with delicate touches, then, with the same soft white comb—her fingers—smoothed his hair. Discovering, in the process, a few gray hairs, she murmured: "Oh, *pobre*! See what I have cost thee!"

Very gently she began to trace and smooth out the lines of worry upon his face, and, rediscovering his cleft chin, she repeated, with a soft laugh, her comment made that night in the shepherd's hut. "Oh, fickle! fickle! I said thy wife would need the sharpest of eyes, but they will needs have nimble fingers that steal thee from me."

Her face at that moment formed a playground for all that was arch, but presently it took the shadow of sadder thoughts. Brimming over, a big tear rolled down her cheek. Yet, while sincerely sorry for Sebastien, she was perfectly frank with herself in thought. "I would not, if I could, bring him back. 'Twould mean only more trouble—for all of us. Now, at least, he is at peace.

"They will think me hard and cruel." Her musings continued. "The whole Barranca will throw up hands of horror—the hands that applauded the greater sin when I gave myself without love in marriage. *Bueno!*" She scornfully tossed her head. "Wicked or not, I will do it—for thee."

She squeezed his face so hard, murmuring it, that he stirred, and for fully a minute thereafter she sat holding her breath. But he slept on. During the last hour the river had widened, and along its banks tufted cocoa palms were woven with the brighter foliage of bananas into the rich green damask of the bordering jungle. Also the sun had prevailed for a few hours in the daily battle with the mists, and under the golden spell of light and warmth the girl's musings grew happier as they floated on. When she awoke him to the sight of the blue harbor opening up from behind a long bend, Seyd looked up at a smiling face.

"That's the American consulate." After rubbing the sleep out of his eyes he pointed out a white stone building which perched, like a gull, on a terrace above the flaming rose and gold of the adobe town. "We'll go there. The consul is a fine old fellow. He'll help us all he can."

First, however, they were destined to encounter the unexpected, for when, an hour later, Seyd pulled the dugout into a ragged wooden pier an officer in the silver and gray of the Mexican rurales pushed through the peon laborers who thronged the wharf.

"You are from up river, señor? Then you can tell us of the flood in the Barranca. A cousin of mine, Don Sebastien—*Caramba!*" At the sight of Francesca he broke suddenly off. "It is surely the señorita Garcia? You will remember me, Eduardo Gallardo, upon the occasion that I visited, at San Nicolas, your uncle, the excellent General Garcia, with my wife, who is of your kinsfolk?"

Recognizing him while he was still in the crowd, Francesca had gained time to prepare. His use of her maiden name proved that here at the port they had heard nothing as yet of her marriage, so, after briefly describing Sebastien's death and the destruction of El Quiss, she concluded: "I was saved by the señor, here, who rode in to warn us. But for him I also should have drowned."

And Seyd availed himself of the opening. "As the señorita is completely exhausted, señor, you will please to excuse us. We go to the American consulate."

"But why the consulate, señor," the rurale politely objected, "when she owns here the house of her kinswoman? The señora, my wife—"

"*Si*, I have heard of her—nothing that is not lovely." Drawing him a little aside, Francesca proceeded to heal, with winning smiles, the wound in his pride. "You shall give her my love, cousin. Tell her that I should prefer to visit her, but, having taken my life from the hand of this señor, I cannot do otherwise than fall in with his plans."

Deferring with Latin politeness to her wish, his pride was none the less hurt, and while they climbed the hill to the consulate he hurried home to his wife, whose feminine intuitions placed the whole matter in an entirely new light.

"A gringo, sayest thou? Then it will be he for whose sake she was sent away to Europe. Medium tall, is he, with a straight nose, hollow cheeks, quick gray eyes? The very man that Paulo, the administrador, described to me on his last visit to the port. *Caramba!* Here's fine bread for the baking! 'Tis told all over the Barranca that she has this man in her blood, and count me for a liar if she comes with him this far for any purpose but marriage. 'Twill never do to have Don Luis knocking at our door to ask why we let her go before our very eyes. He is a power, *hombrecita*, with the government, thy master, and, fail or win, we lose nothing by trying to trip her run. And 'twill be easy! A word in the ear of the *jefe*, judge, and priest, and 'tis done. And do not sleep on it. Away with you—at once."

In his cool white salon on the hill above, the consul—a portly old fellow with a clean, good-natured face—was counseling Seyd at that moment in almost the same terms.

"As you say, this is no time to stand on conventions—especially after the man had locked you in and left you to drown. After seeing the young lady"— his smiling glance went to the door through which Francesca had just gone with his wife—"I should feel less than ever like protracted mourning. Besides, it is now or never. If you don't marry her at once the chance may never come again. If Eduardo Gallardo hadn't seen you it would have been quite simple. I could have fixed it up for you all right. But he is counted

- 144 -

something of a sneak, and if he once sniffs the wind—well, you can be sure he won't let such a chance slip to better himself with General Garcia. You've simply got to beat him to it."

After a pause of thought he went on: "In their usual course, both the legal and ecclesiastical procedures are very slow. It takes about a week for the lawyers to coin the bridegroom's natural impatience into ready money, and after they are through the Church holds out its hand for what's left. It's an awful graft, but has its advantages, for if the wheels are well greased they spin like lightning. Shut up! I don't have to be told that you emerged from the flood with empty pockets. I'll attend to that, and you can settle with me any old time. All you have to do"—taking Seyd by the shoulders, he marched him into his own bedroom—"is to take a shave and bath and make yourself look as much as you can like a happy bridegroom."

With a last order, "Help yourself from my clothes," he went out laughing. But when he returned an hour later his smile was obscured by a vexed cloud. "Eduardo wins," he reported to Seyd, who had just come out on the veranda. "He must have gone right to it, for when I arrived at the *edificio municipal* they were already primed. The judge and *jefe-politico* both count themselves of mine, but they wouldn't do a thing. Really you can't blame them. *El general* Garcia is a name to conjure with down here, and they are all afraid of their official heads. 'Much as we would like to serve you,' and so forth, 'but in the case of a young lady of such high family we dare not proceed without her guardian's written consent.'

"And the *jefe* gave me good advice. *El capitan*, Eduardo, it seems, is not only ambitious, but not a bit too scrupulous about the way by which he gains his ends. So you must not go out alone. It would be quite easy to trump up some charge, arrest, and then shoot you as an escaping prisoner under the law of *El Fuga*. You wouldn't be the first to be shot inside the prison and then thrown outside, and, though I should most certainly hold an inquiry and kick up an awful row, that wouldn't bring you back to life. Also we shall have to look out that they don't kidnap your girl."

While the consul was thus easing his bosom of its load of doubt Seyd had stared out over the blue harbor at a steamer that was taking cargo from a dozen lighters. Suddenly he asked, "What ship is that?"

"The *Curaçao*, of San Francisco."

"American, then. When does she sail?"

"To-morrow morning at five."

"How far outside the harbor does Mexican jurisdiction extend?"

"The usual three miles beyond the headlands."

Seyd came to his point. "Then what is to prevent her skipper from marrying us?"

"*Bueno!*" The consul slapped him on the back. "He'll do it sure, for he's a friend of mine. Bravo! Trust your lover to find a way."

CHAPTER XXVII

Instead of the steps of a church, which form the natural way to their new estate for the great majority of brides, Francesca stepped into hers from the companion ladder of the *Curaçao*. But there had been various happenings—the visit of the Doña Gracio de Gallardo y Garcio to urge, in her own stout black person, Francesca's acceptance of her house and contents, her husband's equally hospitable offer of horses and escort for her safe conduct to San Nicolas, also his subsequent espionage and the means by which they evaded it. And now she was stepping from the companionway into the launch which was to take the newly married pair.

Just as the consul had done his best for Seyd, so, with a woman's natural enthusiasm for a wedding, his wife had dressed the girl. By means of a few pins plus a basting needle a pretty dress had been pulled into a perfect fit, and out of its foam her shapely head now rose like a delicate dark flower. In the dusk of a crushed panama her clear-cut face glowed with unusual color. Swaying there on Seyd's arm, she made a picture which drew the admiration of the men and the tender sympathy of the women passengers who looked down upon them from the rail. While Seyd was handing her into the launch a storm of rice broke overhead and fell softly into the water, and when, leaving them dancing in its wake, the big hulk of the ship moved on, a hearty cheer floated back to them.

If not so boisterous, the congratulations of the consul at the pier were equally hearty. "You didn't do it a bit too soon," he informed them. "Just after you left friend Eduardo notified me that it had been decided in a family council that your wife should go at once to the house of her relative. Without actually saying it he gave me to understand that a charge of kidnapping lay behind the demand. Just for the fun of it I let him wander along, and when I sprang it, and told him that by this time you were undoubtedly married, you should have seen his face. He won't trouble you again—neither will he furnish you horses."

"That doesn't matter," his wife put in. "I have that all arranged."

"What?" The consul looked his surprise. "What's this? A conspiracy? I expected that you would stay with us at least a week?"

"No." His wife took the answer into her own hands. "You know, Francesca's mother and uncle are grieving in the belief that she is drowned. And she has other reasons of her own—and yours," she added for Seyd. "Though you are not to bother her with questions."

At the consulate breakfast was waiting, and in the cheer of the following hour and bustle of departure, Seyd forgot his momentary wonder. It did not revive until, early that afternoon, they reined in to rest their horses on the crest of the first hill in the chain that led in giant steps up to the plateau above the Barranca. As they rode on, after a last look at the harbor, which lay like a huge turquoise within its setting of hills, he looked inquiringly at Francesca.

"Can you not guess?" she asked. When he shook his head she rallied him with a happy laugh upon his dullness. "I think your memory is very poor, Señor Rosario."

"What—Rosa!" For instantly there flashed up a picture of her wet face looking at him from under her capote hood on the day that he found her standing in the rain beside her fallen horse.

"So you recognize me at last?"

"You don't mean to say—"

"*Si*, señor, my husband"—contradicting her laugh, a deep thrill inhered in the words—"it is even so. In the days before the railroad, when there was great travel between San Nicolas and the port, Don Luis maintained houses a day's journey apart. Though none of our family has visited them in the last two years, they were in good condition when Paulo passed this way at the beginning of the rains. So to-night, Rosario, we bide in our own house."

Again did her accent on the "our" move and thrill him. Always undemonstrative, however, he merely caught her hand, and so, linked like children, they rode on side by side. At first they observed a happy silence, but presently the trail took on such remarkable likeness to the one they had traveled that other day, proceeding from the stretches of black volcanic rock through copal and scrub oak to sparsely grassed barrens, that the strength of the associations forced them into talk.

"That's where your horse fell," he began it. When she agreed, he asked, "I wonder if you had any conception of the risks you were running when you rode behind me?"

Though she knew very well what he meant, she pretended ignorance and made him explain in detail his feelings at the sight of her hands resting like white butterflies on the front of his coat, his sudden emotion when the scent of her wet hair floated over his shoulder, utter intoxication whenever a slip of his horse caused her to tighten her hold on his waist.

"You hid it very cleverly," was her comment upon these revelations.

"And you never knew it?"

"Of course I did." To which she added the brazen confession, "Or I would not have done it."

Shooting over a hill not long thereafter, the trail suddenly fell through copal and oak woods into a sheltered valley where, with a suddenness that drew an exclamation of admiration from Seyd, they came in sight of the house. A small adobe, washed with gold with pale-violet borders, it stood under a great banyan tree within the embrace of a grove of tall palms. Almost across its doorway a bright arroyo ran swiftly, to disappear in the dark shade of clump tamarinds. All the afternoon the sun had pursued a futile struggle with the ocean mists, and now, completing the beauty of the place, it shot a last coppery shaft between two clouds.

"A happy augury," was Francesca's greeting to the pathway of light. "Now let it rain."

The door was unlocked, and, entering with her, he found the interior equally to his taste. The solid walls were cream-tinted, and after he had lit the wood which was ready on the open hearth they reflected a comfortable glow on massive tables and chairs of plain oak, wide settees, and roomy lounges. His satisfaction was complete when she told him that it stood alone. The knowledge that they would be barred by leagues of distance, shut in by the rainy night from the rest of the world, filled him with deep content. From a survey, conscious of warmth and comfort, his satisfied gaze returned to the fingers which were fluttering like white butterflies from button to button down her raincoat.

"Lazy one!" She spoke with a pretty assumption of wifely authority. "Stable the horses—but first bring in the bundle from my crupper. While you are out I shall prepare our meal."

"What! Do we really eat? How thoughtful! It had never occurred to me."

"A pretty beginning," she made demure answer, "for a wife to starve her husband."

Neither could there be any complaint of the meal that faced him on his return, for it represented the best that could be bought or borrowed by the consul's wife. Afterward Seyd would have washed the dishes, but, taking him by the shoulders, Francesca marched him back to the fire.

"No, I shall do it myself. Please?" She headed off the mutiny betrayed by his eyes. "If you knew how often I have peeped into our work-folks' adobes at night to watch, with envy, some little peona preparing her man's meal, you would understand." So, smoking by the fire, he watched with huge comfort the play of dimples in her arms and the fluttering of the small hands which seemed so hopelessly at odds with their task.

While working she chattered happily, but after the last dish was ranged in the plate rack on the wall she came to him and sank in a graceful heap beside his chair. Head pillowed on one white arm spread across his knee, she gazed thoughtfully into the fire; and, looking down upon her, Seyd's thought reverted once more to the shepherd's hut. Again he had difficulty in realizing that it was indeed he, Robert Seyd, mining engineer, who was sharing food and fire with this, his wife, daughter on one side of a proud Spanish house and on the other of descent that ran back into the dim time of the Aztecs.

Her voice called him out of his wonder, and while the fire leaped and crackled in defiance of the wind and rain without they talked of this and that, their trials and travail, absent thoughts, hopes; and in the telling of it they obtained surcease from the smart of past misunderstandings. Also there were confessions. Each told—she with a blush—how they had overlooked each other's sleep in the shepherd's hut. Because opportunity for such communion had been altogether lacking, they talked late. Their murmurs died with the last light of the fire.

CHAPTER XXVIII

At high noon two days thereafter Seyd and Francesca drew rein on the rim of the Barranca above San Nicolas.

During the moment that the horses rested their thoughts reverted to the last occasion when they had overlooked the great void, and if the thought of Sebastien brought a touch of sadness into the girl's reflections it caused no bitterness. She turned with a low laugh when Seyd produced from an inner pocket the handkerchief he had picked up that day on the trail.

"It did," she said, when he told how it seemed to drip tears. "I had cried all the way up the trail to the rim."

After the usual nightly downpour the sun had come out, and under a flood of golden light the valley floor stood out in relief, with its wooded hills and hollows diminished to toy proportions by the awful depth. In the center the *casa* of San Nicolas sat like a gold cup in the wide green saucer of surrounding pastures. Beyond, the river lay, a band of fretted silver, splitting the valley; and, following its course upward, the girl's eye paused at the yellow scar, high on the opposite wall, which marked Santa Gertrudis.

"My beacon on many a dark day." She pointed.

"And that reminds me that it is in great danger of being extinguished," Seyd answered. "Our first payment was due the day before yesterday. Unless Billy has returned in my absence with the money—and I haven't the slightest hope—the property is forfeited to your uncle."

"But he will not claim it." Out of her simple woman's faith she went on: "He is too good and kind to advantage himself by your misfortune. In spite of his hate for the gringos, he likes you personally. Now that you are—my husband, he will not attempt your harm."

In view of his present clear view of Don Luis's machinations, Seyd was not so sure. Unwilling to hurt her, he conceded: "Well, we shall see. Let us ride on down."

"Not together, dear." Leaning over, she caught his arm. "I must see him first alone. He will be furiously angry, of course. But the angrier the better, for just so much sooner will follow the calm."

"But he may try—"

"—To take me from you?" She took the words out of his mouth. "He cannot. In a day, a week, a month, sooner or later, I should escape. They could not forever keep me locked up. But he will not try. You know, he stole his own wife, snatched her away while she was going to church to marry another, and he comes of a race that gained wives as often as not by the sword. He cannot blame you without condemning himself, and I am sure that he will not try. If you give me a little time to conquer him and soothe my poor scandalized mother it will come out all right. So you must go on to Santa Gertrudis now and see if there be any news of Señor Thornton. And to-morrow—you may come."

"If you have the slightest doubt"—loath to let her out of his hands, he hesitated—"I would ride on to the station. Beautiful as is this place, and much as I have come to love it, I would rather abandon all than incur the risk."

"But there is none, husband mine." She looked up in his face, tenderly smiling. "He will rage and roar like an old lion, but that is all. I should be only half a woman to have come to my age without learning to manage him. Remember, for the second time you have saved my life, and, being already married, he cannot deny us. So go in peace, and"—she put up her mouth— "love."

In spite of her reassurance, he watched her go with apprehension that took a blacker tinge when, arriving at the inn late in the afternoon, he found no word from Billy. Though the inn's meager accommodations had not been improved by a slap from the wing tip of the wave, he remained there all night in preference to crossing and recrossing the river. With so much at stake, Santa Gertrudis could take care of itself for another day. Sleeping with anxiety for a bedfellow, he rose and was on the road at daybreak—but not a bit earlier than Francesca, who met him halfway.

"I knew you would be anxious," she explained, "so I saddled a horse and stole away while all of San Nicolas was still asleep. But not for nothing are you to have my news. *Si*, it is good!

"'Twas as I said," she went on, having received her reward. "The *madre* had already cried herself beyond further tears, and was glad to have me on any terms. The good uncle, of course, stormed. Never was there such a battle since the French wars, and had you been there 'twould not have lacked its killed and wounded. Until midnight we fought; then, after cursing the blood of the Irishman that has always led me astray, he gave in. ''Tis not for an old soldier to cross tongues with a woman,' he growled. 'To-morrow bring me thy man.' But he knew that he was beaten," she finished, confidently, "for when I kissed him he laughed in his throat and patted my hair."

Again Seyd refused to dash her hope, but he was not quite convinced, and when they entered the big living-room where Don Luis stood with Paulo in waiting his dark gravity cast its shadow over the girl's glad face. His immobility afforded no clue to the feeling that lay behind the stereotyped greeting, "The house, señor, is yours.

"I am the more pleased to see you," he went on, "because Paulo reminded me an hour ago of a matter of business that lies between us. Such things stick not in my memory. But I believe it concerns some money."

"Señor!" Her face flaming with the scarlet of shame, Francesca was moving forward.

He stopped her with a shake of his heavy head. "This is between me and— your husband. The papers, Paulo. Hand them to the señor."

It was a legal process, signed and sealed according to Mexican law, and before opening it Seyd knew it for the end. More out of curiosity than for information, he rapidly scanned the terms which had taken Santa Gertrudis and its mined riches forever out of his hands. While he read, Don Luis studied his face. If he looked for signs of deep hurt there were none to be seen, for in the long game between them Seyd was confronted for the first time by the expected. He looked up, squaring his shoulders.

"The victory is yours, señor."

To Francesca's anxious eyes it seemed that the old man's gravity lightened by a shade. "You will concede, señor, that I warned you—that no gringo would ever force himself in on my lands?"

"Yes, and I did my best to disprove it. For my partner's sake I am sorry. For my own"—he looked at his wife—"I am glad."

"Well spoken, señor." The shadow of a smile illumined the old man's dark reserve. "But if I warned you, it does not follow that I have not watched with some sympathy your struggle. In watching, too, my old eyes have been opened upon truths that I had refused to see, though they lay under my nose. We are an old people, señor, we Mexicans. The old blood of Spain added no effervescence to the Aztec strains that were grown stagnant long before Cortez landed, and when a people ages nature removes it to make way for younger stock. *Si*, though I refused to acknowledge it, I have known many years that just as the Moors overran Spain, and the Spanish overran the Aztecs, so will your people overrun Mexico from the Northern Sierras to the Gulf.

"Once I had thought to stay it. But time cools the hottest blood, and the one I had counted upon to uphold my old hands is gone to his place forever. Also I have seen that no man can dam the tide or shut the gates that Porfirio Diaz opened. As it went with Texas and Alta California so will it go with all our states. Against your Yankee our softer people can never stand. In the time to come only those of us that mix blood with shrewder strains will be able to withstand the flood, and thus it is I, who would have killed once the man that said I should ever take a gringo for kinsman, accept you with resignation. Perhaps it is the easier because one such mixture gave us this bright girl. And if you took time by the forelock 'tis not for me to grumble. One word more—" He threw one arm around Francesca, who had crossed to his side. "It has never been the habit of the Garcias to overlook a good dower to one of the house, and the fact that my niece has given you herself in exchange for her life does not cancel *my* debt. Give me the papers. The others, Paulo—to the señor."

While Seyd gazed at the title deeds to Santa Gertrudis, made out to himself and Billy, the old man slowly tore up the forfeiture. Applying a match to the pieces, he threw them on the hearth, and, blazing up, they added warmth to the grim smile that accompanied his words.

"I told you, señor, that no gringo should ever *force* himself in on my land."

THE END

Milton Keynes UK
Ingram Content Group UK Ltd.
UKHW010850010724
444982UK00005B/508